SHORTS FROM

SURREY

Edited by

SUZI BLAIR

NEW FICTION

First published in 1993 by
NEW FICTION
4 Hythegate, Werrington
Peterborough,
PE4 7ZP

Printed in Great Britain by Forward Press.

Foreword

The advent of New Fiction signifies the expansion of what has traditionally been, a limited platform for writers of short stories. New Fiction aims to promote new short stories to the widest possible audience.

The *Shorts* collections represent the wealth of new talent in writing, and provide enjoyable, interesting and readable stories appealing to a diversity of tastes.

Intriguing and entertaining; from sharp character sketches to 'slice of life' situations, the stories have been selected because each one is *a good read*.

This collection of short stories is from the pens of the people of Surrey. They are new stories, sweeping across the spectrums of style and subject to reflect the richness of character intrinsic to the region, today.

Suzi Blair
Editor.

Contents

Playing Host

by

Mike Swaddling

'... all of which brings me to last night. How the writing got on the wall I don't know. I don't think I dreamt, and as far as I know, I spent a peaceful night. The flat is alarmed and no-one can have got in.

But I don't really care. None of it matters now, anyway. It's all too far gone.

It's cool out here on the balcony. I wonder how it will feel. I'm getting tense but it's the only way now. Everything's a mess. I wonder if I'll say anything beforehand. I'll probably think it's the bloke in the flat below. I'll wave as I pass...'

Harris stared at the final words. Then, without saying anything to his companion, he went back to the beginning and started again.

'The first time it happened, I was on a bus. I was on my way to an interview, in heavy traffic, and stuck at lights with twenty minutes to go. I was trying to calm down. Arriving flustered would be a lousy start. Through the lights and fifty yards round the corner there was a request stop. If no-one was there, I would be OK.

At first it looked as if I was in luck, but at the last moment, out of a doorway stepped an old man, and stuck out his arm. The bus pulled up rather sharply. Instead of getting on, he disappeared back into the doorway, and slowly re-emerged with a woman of the same age, clearly quite frail. He guided her onto the bus and left her while he went back, reappearing with two heavy suitcases, and struggling up the steps.

It got worse. The old boy only had a fiver, and the driver had no change. He turned to his companion, who had remained exactly where he had left her, like a Tussauds exhibit, and asked if she had anything smaller.

She slowly came to life, and started looking for her handbag. It was hanging on her arm. I glanced again at my watch, and felt a surge of panic as she fumbled for her purse. I raised my eyes, and silently asked the Grand Instigator why he was doing this to me. Why? Why?

As if in response, the man in front of me spoke.

1

'Oh, get a move on, you dozy old pair!' The bus went silent.

'Well done,' I thought. 'Someone's spoken out.' To my surprise, however, the couple across the gangway turned and looked at me. So did the girls in front of them and, astoundingly, so did the man in front who had just spoken. And I heard mutterings from the seats behind. I shifted uneasily in my seat, cleared my throat and stared in the supermarket window. Why were they looking at me?

The old couple sat down. I was late for the interview. I didn't get the job.

Ten days later I was at the cinema. Next to me was Janice from the youth club, who had been the object of my affection for some time.

I forget the film. My memory has probably blocked it out in a vain attempt to forget the whole painful incident. I can only remember this young couple up on the screen, in a car. I vaguely recall him putting an arm around her shoulder.

Then the chap in front suddenly yelled, 'Go on, sunshine, give her one!'

There was another silence, then Janice stormed up the aisle and out of my life. I remained seated, stunned beyond movement. Again I sensed the eyes of everyone were on me, not on the seat in front.

My first thought was to check the person in front of me. But from the back he looked completely different from the one on the bus, so that was that theory up the spout. I crept out of the cinema.

After that it all becomes a blur. Apparently I told my night school tutor to stop boring everyone before I stuffed his textbook down his throat, a policeman in a traffic jam warned me for using foul language with the sun-roof open, and what supposedly happened in the supermarket queue is not something I would care to talk about.

Then the inevitable happened. I had virtually become a recluse, cancelling all social activities. But I still had my job and I had to work. Fortunately I was in an office by myself, without much contact with people. Until the staff meeting.

Attendance was not compulsory, but everyone knew that absences were noted. Again, it seemed to me that it was the chap in front that told the Managing Director that the latest accounts should be entered for the Booker Fiction Prize, and that no-one in the company thought he could make a salad in a greengrocers. But I had long stopped believing what I thought happened.

I am told that I handled the situation reasonably well. Jim on the gate gave a sympathetic smile as I left. But at the end of the day I had no job, no friends and no social life. Mum rang that evening and asked why they hadn't seen me for six weeks. I didn't have the courage to tell her...'

Harris slid the scrawled sheets back across the table.

'Did you see this writing on the wall?'

'I did,' said Detective Sergeant Lambert to the reporter. 'And it's not something I'll forget in a hurry.'

'Why? What did it say?'

'It wasn't so much the words... more the handwriting.'

'How do you mean?'

'It was weird. Like that old fashioned German writing, you know...'

'Gothic?'

'That's it. Like you see in churches.'

'Odd,' said Harris, doodling a very ornate 'G'. 'What did it say?'

'Here.' Lambert pushed his own notepad across the table. In a handwriting that Harris noted could probably not be much further removed from the original, he read:

'None see me arrive, none see me leave. I am weary and go to rest before I seek another Host. Farewell. You amuse me no longer. 'Twas the same with each one before.'

Whispers

by

Caroline Jane Beaton

I am Dominic, Guardsman 2564H212, and as I write, I am drowning in Falling-bostel. I write this journal as I think - no - fear it is my only means of express-ion; self expression.

Here this night lay some thirty-seven other men, yet I am alone in the dark-ness and alone in my mind. Never do I think more than in times of depression... I am drowning; drowning in my own rancid philosophies; rancid so I am told - yet not one of my colleagues will save me. Not that they could (I laugh).

This unit is my 'home'. I am incredibly alone. The whole concept of militar-ism is a mind-game, I being a pawn in their strategy of discipline and that in itself a composite of ranking egotists; an anathema to my very existence.

I am a uniform; a number; a cliché. God knows I've suffered the torments of khaki long enough, imprisoned in its ideals. For three years they have imposed their beliefs on mine and although my face greets them with an expressionless façade, my mind groans with revulsion when their concepts are thrust upon it.

A dead fly crushed against the window catches my eye; a colleague stirs (I yawn), yet no nearer am I to that semi-conscious world of escapism.

Have you noticed how the whole world survives - no - thrives on communi-cation? We all need to communicate: to speak, to listen, to watch, to touch - to be touched...

I have so many ideas, feelings; thoughts of which to tell; thoughts that are mere whispers in my subconscious mind, sometimes breaking through into my conscious mode of thinking. My colleagues do not share my fashion of thought or want of expression. I have taken to silence when in their presence. I am con-sidered 'the weird shit in bunk 27' (I smile). My thoughts are with my existence and not with any learned ability to conquer the egos of others. I often lay here awake, absorbing my surroundings, just thinking - self acquaintance, untar-nished by my rank or number... my mind - my sanctuary.

At six I will rise. At six-thirty I will breakfast. At seven I will parade. Come mid-evening I will make my way to the telephone box; itself the very sarcopha-gus of communication and willingly entomb myself within its glass walls. There I will lift the receiver and grab briefly at reality. I will dial London. I will speak, listen, then speak again - but I will not watch, nor will I touch or be touched. There is no touch for a lonely man.

I am Dominic, Guardsman 2564H212, and as I write I am drowning in Fallingbostel: I'm alone.

The Solitary Bullet

by

Edward Hodgkinson

'Did you bring your share of the money?' asked Dickson.

'Yeah, I brought it,' replied Rogers. 'Did you?'

'Yes, you don't think I'd con you, do you?'

'No. Okay, let's get on with it.'

Both men put the black leather briefcases they were carrying onto the wooden table, which apart from the two chairs on either side of the table were the only furniture in the drab attic room, and then opened them. Both briefcases contained ten piles of a thousand made up of a hundred pound notes.

'Ten thousand each, like we agreed,' said Dickson. He removed a snub-nosed .38 revolver from the inside pocket of his black overcoat, swung the cylinder out of the frame, inserted a bullet into one of the six empty chambers, spun the cylinder, snapped it back into the frame and then placed the revolver on the table.

'All set,' he said. 'The one who survives keeps the money. Does anyone know that you're here? The reason why I chose this dump is that the landlord down-stairs wouldn't ask any questions if you paid him enough. He's had plenty of shifty characters in here to know when to keep his mouth shut.'

'Shifty characters?' asked Rogers. 'What do you take me for? I'm a busines-sman. And nobody knows that I'm here, I'm not that stupid.'

'It pays to be cautious. We don't want people to know what we're up to, do we? Especially the police.'

'No, we don't. Who will get rid of the body?'

Dickson smiled. 'When the landlord hears the shot he will wait five minutes for the survivor to leave and then he will dispose of the body. The police will never know that anything has happened.'

'I'm impressed, you've planned this well.'

'Thank you. Shall we get on with it?'

'Okay, you go first.'

Rogers picked up the revolver, his eyes never leaving Dickson's face. He turned it over in his hands and then sat down on one of the chairs. Dickson sat down in the chair opposite him, with the table between them. The feeling of hatred was mutual between them, but neither of them would say anything to each other. Dickson had known from the first moment when he had met Rogers that there was something evil about him. He was the type of person that people crossed the street to avoid. A dangerous misfit who took big risks, not caring about the consequences. It was obvious that he had done this sort of thing before and that made Dickson edgy. He had suggested playing a game of Russian roulette as a joke and Rogers had agreed if the stakes were high enough. Dickson wasn't sure whether he wanted to get involved with Rogers or to stay clear of him, but the money involved was too much to ignore if he survived. He had no family and no close friends, so he wouldn't be missed if he lost. It was the biggest gamble of all, but he was prepared to risk it.

Rogers put the revolver barrel against his head and smiled, his eyes spelling pure evil. 'Here goes,' he said and chuckled. Dickson's flesh began to creep with the thought of Rogers being so casual about something so deadly. He wished that the bullet would be in the first chamber and then it would be all over. He would be able to take the money and not worry about the consequences. Rogers slowly squeezed the trigger...

Click.

Rogers grinned and chuckled again. 'Your turn,' he said. He put the gun on the table, reached inside his overcoat and removed a carton of cigarettes and a lighter. He lit one of the cigarettes and blew a stream of smoke towards the ceiling.

Dickson felt revolted at the way that Rogers was acting as if he knew that no harm would come to him, but now it was his turn and his thoughts changed to nothing but his own survival. He picked up the revolver, gripping the handle with a sweaty, trembling hand; his eyes never leaving Rogers' face. His opponent's eyes were hypnotically evil. There was a lifetime of cruelty and corruption in those eyes; never showing any pity, shame or remorse. Dickson wanted to turn the gun on him, but he didn't have the guts to murder a man, unlike his opponent. He put the barrel to his head, feeling the cold steel. Shivers ran up and down his spine as he cocked the revolver, waiting the timeless moment for the expectant bullet to ricochet through his skull. He tried not to show his fear, but he knew that Rogers could sense it and was laughing at him for being so weak. He felt his heart pounding in his chest and his blood rushing madly in his ears. He closed his eyes and pulled the trigger...

Click.

Dickson opened his eyes, but he didn't need to see to know that Rogers had been smiling all along. He put the gun on the table, his body shaking convulsively.

Rogers picked up the revolver, still grinning like a Cheshire cat. 'You know,' he said. 'I thought you were a goner for a minute. Still, plenty of time for that to happen. My turn.' He fingered the cylinder and barrel, massaging the droplets of sweat into the dark steel and then stared at the dirty mark on the tip of his index finger with great fascination. 'Your hands are very sweaty,' he said. 'You aught to try and calm down. After all, it may be all over in a minute.' He chuckled again, knowing that it would unnerve Dickson even more. He put the barrel to his head, still smiling and staring at Dickson, cocked it and squeezed the trigger slowly...

Click.

'Isn't this fun,' he said. 'And it's almost over. Your turn.' He put the revolver on the table and took a long drag on his cigarette.

Dickson picked up the gun slowly, touching it tentatively with his fingertips at first as if it was red hot, then gripping the handle and lifting the revolver with his trembling hand. He was scared now, so scared. Beads of sweat trickled down his face as he tried to hold the gun steady against his head. He screwed his eyes tightly shut again, cocked the revolver, gritted his teeth and pulled the trigger...

Click.

Dickson wanted to be sick. He put the revolver back on the table and watched as Rogers picked it up, cocked it, and pointed the barrel into his open mouth; tempting death to blow his brains out. Dickson longed to see Roger's head explode, splattering fragments of bone and brain all over the room; a chance to see that smug smile wiped off his face forever; no more evil eyes...

Click.

Dickson wanted to scream. Rogers had won; the evil bastard had won. He looked at the revolver on the table and then at Rogers. Tears began to run down his face, his body shuddering with fear. 'I can't do it,' he blubbered. 'I can't.'

Rogers chuckled, but his face was deadly serious now. 'Oh, but you must. We made a deal and now you must fulfil your part. It'll only take a second.'

Dickson shook his head and fell to his knees in front of Rogers. 'I can't do it. Take the money and let me live. I won't say anything. We'll never see each other again, I promise. Please, just don't make me do it.'

Rogers chuckled. 'I'm sorry. I can't take that risk. We made a deal.' He removed a .38 revolver from inside his overcoat, swung out the cylinder, placed a

8

bullet in one of the chambers, spun the cylinder and then snapped it back into the frame.

'What are you doing?' Dickson asked frantically. 'Please let me live.'

Rogers pushed the revolver barrel into Dickson's open mouth. 'I'm sorry, but you lose.' He cocked it and squeezed the trigger...

Click.

He did it again despite Dickson's pleading and begging...

Click.

And again...

Click.

And again...

Bang!

Robes and Wigs

by

Robin F Lawrence

It was a poorly lit room on the top floor of the local education equipment centre. Countless shelves of theatrical paraphernalia gave one the sense of being in another world. Here was an amazing conglomeration of hats, cloaks, robes, wigs, masks and a hundred and one other necessities for local schools' stage productions. A gay cavalier figure vied for the limelight with an elegant Elizabethan. There were selections of roundlet hats, doublets, bonnets, puffed sleeves and many other extras.

Sadly, the collection was little used. Visitors, although impressed by the wide range of items for hire, seldom returned for some reason or another.

Miss Garside was the lady in charge of the collection and was totally dedicated to her job, seldom having any leave, which would have meant entrusting her prized possession to another member of the centre's staff. To say she was eccentric would have been kind. She was a portly woman in her early fifties with bulging eyes and what appeared to be a wig far too young for her. Her favourite colour was black and it often camouflaged her against the background of dark costumes, resulting occasionally in a visiting teacher being taken by surprise when moving along the narrow aisles between the packed shelves.

It was a Wednesday afternoon early in the autumn term when a young teacher, fresh from training college, approached room number four hundred and one on the top floor of the equipment centre. The door was clearly marked:

Costume Section   Head of Section: Miss L Garside

He approached with a high degree of expectancy. Mathematics and French textbooks were dull fare compared to drama class aids and equipment. He knocked and entered. There was little room to manoeuvre. He said, 'Hello,' hesitantly as he could see nobody present.

Just as he was about to take himself around the collection there was a movement on the other side of the room. Miss Garside introduced herself dramatically, attired in a recently acquired Tudor head-dress.

'A thousand welcomes to you, young sir,' she cried.

He laughed, self-consciously.

10

'I was beginning to think I would have no visitors today. I am so glad you came. Have you a particular interest?'

'No. I just wanted to have a browse around. I only began teaching full-time this term.'

He was surprised to find her locking the door behind them.

'I won't have time for any other visitors today.'

'Oh, I won't keep you long.' He was beginning to feel uneasy and his initial interest in the collection was evaporating fast. 'She's as mad as a hatter,' he thought to himself.

'Perhaps we will start in what I like to call the horror section,' she suggested.

'Oh, sure, yes. Why not?' He sounded as agreeable as he could.

She put on a grotesque mask and leered at him.

'Children love this sort of thing. The more gruesome the better as far as they're concerned.'

He managed to direct his glance elsewhere.

She pulled down from a shelf what appeared to be a witch's broom stick and proceeded to 'ride' on it up the passage.

'It's a shame it's not made for two,' she playfully remarked. He was un-amused.

A glittering silver-papered wooden sword caught her attention and she made out to fence him with it. 'Ahoy.'

His manner changed rapidly from one of unease to one of exasperation. 'Look here,' he fumed. 'Open that door and let me out. I've got better ways of spending my time. You're mad.'

'I'm what? What did you say?'

She was obviously hurt.

So much so that he not only faced a barrage of verbal abuse but an aerial bombardment of every item she could lay her hands on. Boxes, hats, wigs, false noses and all kinds of make-up came hurtling his way.

He was only of slight stature but lacked nothing in courage. 'Hand me the key,' he demanded, standing his ground.

She pushed past him, strode to the door and unlocked it. 'You haven't heard the last of this, young man, I promise you.'

And he had not. By the Friday morning his headmistress had a serious complaint on her desk, accusing him of conduct unbecoming a school teacher. Miss Garside had cuts and bruises to prove it.

In spite of the strongest appeals, he was flabbergasted to find himself in no time at all dismissed from the teaching profession.

He appealed vehemently to the head of the equipment centre, the teachers' union and the local education authority. But he could convince no-one. They just could not believe his version of the incident.

I could. I am Miss Garside.

Albert's Shed

by

H Hutchin

Every Saturday morning, Albert spent hours in the potting shed, down near Castleton Street. In fact for thirty years, no one had been able to touch him for his Geraniums. His wife had died over twenty years ago, one minute she had been there, the next she had vanished, so neighbours said. Nobody knew much about her.

Albert was a very tidy man, wanting everything in its place. Although retired now from his long time portering job at the local hospital, he still liked gardening and tidying up. All the Geraniums he grew were perfect, all planted out in dead straight lines. Now and again he would take them to the local market and sell them for a good price, then with the money buy more seeds and cuttings. He didn't have many friends, his friends were his flowers. Drinking, gambling and women didn't mean anything to him, he just wanted a nice tidy life.

Nobody knew about the mistake he had once made when just a slip of a boy. He had gone with some pals to a local hop, and there had been this girl, laughing and smiling, with brown hair and lovely hazel eyes. Albert, although shy, had been drawn to her from the first moment he had seen her. They had married a year later. Rosie, he called her although her real name was Rosemary Calvert.

Living in Castleton Street, near the big hospital where he worked, had been convenient, and they had soon settled down to wedded bliss. Rosie hadn't worked, in those days wives stayed at home.

As the years flew by, Rosie had begun to get fed up. Unknown to Albert, she would pop down to the Jug and Bottle and buy a bottle of stout now and then. It had soon become a bad habit.

Albert's dinners had gradually got less tasty, the meat underdone, the potatoes cold, his favourite steak and kidney pudding had tasted of rubber. He didn't know why, but he had begun to shout at her, telling her she had all day at home, surely a decent dinner wasn't too much to ask of her? Rosie had been getting fatter and bloated looking, her make-up all in a jumble on the dressing table, her underclothes all in a heap on the floor. Albert's socks and pants were

13

not washed for weeks, and when he wanted a clean shirt, there was never a clean one to put on. It had all begun to get on his nerves.

Thinking back all those years, nobody would have guessed that Rosie hadn't died a natural death. Living alone after twenty years, the lifestyle suited Albert. He could please himself, no questions asked.

One day a letter plopped through the door of number thirty-nine, addressed to Mr Albert Squires. It was from the local council, and said that they wished to pull down the old allotments at Castleton Street to make way for a brand new Supermarket which was sorely needed in the area. At the news, shock and horror filled Albert, all those years of pottering in his shed, all his prize flowers, his wallflowers, his dahlias.

He immediately wrote to Bramley Council, telling them that the locals didn't want any of their new fangled Supermarkets, and demanding to know what they supposed was to become of all the smallholdings, especially hut number twenty-nine.

In May the bulldozers came to flatten Albert's shed and the six others which had stood there since the 'dig for victory' days of the last war. They had to hurry, the contract had to be finished by August, when 'Victor Values' Superstore would rise up and give all of Bramley a new lift. Housewifes would be so grateful after all those dirty, dingy shops with cats sitting on the cabbages at old Bashfords, the greengrocers. After all, they deserved something new and exciting.

The foreman of W P Bullen had to leave off work on the Wednesday. Somebody said he had had a nasty shock, they had had to take him to hospital. Someone said he'd seen a corpse near Albert's hut, and in its claw-like hand it had clutched a Gin bottle!

This is the Modern World

by

Andrew Ng

By the time I returned to the car park it was nearly empty. I pressed the 'call lift' button and waited - and waited. Did nothing in this damned city work?

I cursed and looked around the graffiti stricken entrance of this multi-storey 'mausoleum'. The cold concrete floor, still wet from the trail of people returning from the rain soaked streets was littered with cigarette butts. Carelessly discarded McDonalds' wrappers confirmed an evening meal while splattered vomit in one corner confirmed too much beer. A grubby, half torn poster announced a blues band playing a nearby pub six months ago. It's now a brasserie with piped music and a smart young business type clientele. The stink of urine conspired with the vomit and threatened to make me retch while Dave proclaimed his love for Sharon from every wall around me - Cupid and his spray can. After all, this is the modern world.

With the dull steel doors refusing to open, I had no option but to take the stairs. My car was on the fifth level. Stepping around the abandoned beer cans, the smell of urine seemed to rise with every step. I tried in vain to hold my breath and I cursed this place once more. The depressing feel of the place thrust forward the negative images of any large city: indifference, darkness and dampness; dark alleys and damp back streets and warehouses, derelict and forgotten - city wastelands.

How prosperous a city this was, I thought. Urgent and throbbing by day and vibrant and colourful by night. Yet beyond the flirting neon and round the corner from the wine bars and restaurants, lurking, decaying, dying; the grey, the colourless and the forgotten. The other side of the shiny coin, where fetid dogs probed and overturned rubbish bins and tired eyes peered out through grimy windows. Existence. Where worn boots peeped out from beneath torn cardboard and whisky bottles slept in brown paper bags. Pavement paupers, cardboard city...

Level five. I pushed open the door that led from staircase to parking lot. Bazza had been here, it said so on the door. Dave still loved Sharon, this was his mountain top to shout from - true love knows no height, I mused, Spurs 'rooled' and the Rebel Posse had been and gone.

The door stayed open as I walked into the lot. The mechanism was broken, it probably had been for months. The wind would blow it shut, I thought. I felt no inclination to shut it myself. Yellow lines, faded and peeling marked out the parking spaces. My car was at the far end of this tomb, brand new, shiny and red, looking for all the world like a blot on this God-forsaken landscape. Instinctively, I took a quick look around the dimly lit lot lest any muggers be waiting to assault the owner of this new car as he fumbled for his keys. All clear. That is, except for the familiar fast food wrappers and discarded drinks cans and carelessly tossed 'Pay and Display' parking tickets.

A curious thought struck me: that's exactly what we do with ourselves; our cars, our homes, our lives - everything. We pay and display. Our lives are determined by slick adverts and production lines. We're judged by the age of our cars, judged by our houses and neighbourhoods - and convicted by the same: too old, too small, too bad. This is the modern world and healthy means wealthy. And then we wonder why people steal and why the crime rate is rising. Are we all just dead spirits in a material world? Who knows? I thought. And does anyone really care anyway?

I reached the car and opened the door. I was sick of this place. I had been in high spirits but now I was depressed. I wanted to drive and drive until I was far, far away. As far away as possible from this place and the neglect and resentment that spread like a cancer, dark and insidious, the evil within: lurking, decaying, dying.

I glanced over to the back wall to see a youth and a spray can. There in big red letters, a declaration:

'Sharon Is A Slag'

He threw the can against the wall and walked angrily towards me, towards the door. His eyes glowered and his tensed shoulders and clenched fists lent a menacing look to his casual, slightly scruffy appearance of baggy jeans and loose T-shirt. He saw me looking but was unconcerned. Instead, as he passed me, and as if by way of explanation, he just muttered, 'She took what she could, while she could.' Then he was at the staircase and gone.

I leaned against the car and sighed a long and hopeless sigh. Staring vacantly at the wall, the boy's words echoed around my head and I found myself shaking slightly. Finally, I got into the car and started the engine. I was sick of this place. I wanted to drive and drive until I was far, far away...

Three's a Crowd

by

Jack Foster

Stella Hargreaves stood at the gate and waved goodbye to her husband, Stanley, as he cycled down the lane towards the river on his usual Thursday afternoon fishing expedition. When he had turned the corner and disappeared from her sight, she turned and made her way slowly back into the little cottage which had been their home for nearly forty years, and her eyes filled with tears at the thought of how soon, and why, their life together might end.

She opened the front door which led directly into the lounge, and made her way across the room to the cupboard at the side of the fireplace, from which she took out her box of photographs. Moving to the table by the window, she sat down and began to look through the contents of the box, recalling memories from long ago as she saw, again, the tall, strong figure of the young man who stood proudly by her side outside the church, and the tears flowed again as she looked at the photographs of their three children, now married, with their own families, and wondered what they would say when she told them what she knew about their father.

Gazing through the window, but not seeing the view, Stella tried to come to terms with the situation, by going over in her mind the events of the past few days.

Stanley had been, on one or two occasions recently, uncharacteristically evasive, suddenly leaving the house and riding off on that bike of his without telling her where he was going; something that had never happened in all their years together.

Hot, scalding tears ran down her cheeks as she recalled the night, just four days ago, when she heard Stanley, her faithful husband, who up until then had never even looked at another woman, repeat a name over and over in his sleep. There was also the mystery of the money, a large amount of money, that had been taken from their savings account; something that she had only accidentally noticed, as she normally didn't bother to look, preferring to leave such things to Stanley. But she would keep a close eye on things from now on, oh yes! He wasn't going to spend their money on some floozie called Florence.

'Florence,' she thought scornfully. 'Florence the floozie. Who does he think he is, Zebedee?'

Stella tried to imagine what Florence would be like, and decided that she would probably be a pathetic, helpless, whining individual with a voice like a cat having its tail pulled; a parasitic harpy with a scraggy neck around which she would probably be wearing a necklace of cheap beads that had been picked up in some jumble sale. But even as she built up, in her mind, a most unflattering picture of Florence whatever-her-name-was as a cross between Olive Oyl and a pantomime witch, she knew that Stanley could never be attracted by anyone so unattractive, and that the other woman was probably a raving beauty, although she hadn't seen anyone locally who could possibly be the mysterious Florence.

He must be really besotted by her, she thought, as she realized that Stanley had lied to her yet again, by telling her he was going fishing. He couldn't have gone fishing - his rod was still in the corner of the room, where it had been for the last three days.

How could he possibly expect to get away with his lies and clumsy evasions?

Only yesterday, he had said that he had to go into town on business. On business that he refused to discuss with her! They had never had secrets in all their years together, and when she had asked him about the business, for which he had to leave her yet again, for the whole afternoon, he had smiled secretively and tapped the end of his nose with a forefinger.

And now he had gone again, probably to see his other woman. The old fool! How could he hope to keep a secret like that from her? He'd talked in his sleep ever since they were first married - had even joked about it a time or two, saying that he would never dare look at another woman!

It seemed an age since she had heard him, in the early hours, mumbling in his sleep yet again. Most of the time it was garbled nonsense to which she paid little or no attention, but just as she had decided to try and ignore his voice and go to sleep, the words came loud and clear.

'Florence, beautiful Florence, I'll be seeing you soon.'

Shocked by what she had just heard, Stella had got out of bed and gone down to the kitchen, where she had made herself a cup of tea - more for something to do than because she wanted a drink - and sat down to collect her thoughts. Could she have been mistaken? Had she been dreaming that she had heard Stanley talking in his sleep?

At four-thirty, after being unable to decide whether or not she had heard correctly the name, Florence, as people who talked in their sleep didn't always speak clearly (and Stanley did tend to mumble) Stella returned to bed and found her husband sleeping quietly.

That had been on Sunday night, she remembered, and on the Monday morning Stanley had gone out on his bike at nine-thirty, and had not returned until late afternoon. He never went out on a Monday, and in answer to her enquiry had merely told her that he had been over at Tadnorton, a town fifteen miles away, dealing with some urgent matter about which, he had said, she would know, one day soon.

Then again, on Tuesday night, or rather, in the early hours of Wednesday morning, she heard Stanley utter the name, Florence. There could be no mistake! Now, she knew that she wasn't dreaming - Stanley had another woman. How could he?

And now, Stella thought, she had to decide what to do. Could she leave Stanley after all this time, as she had thought she might, or should she fight to save her marriage?

She decided to fight. Why should she just give in? After all she thought, a lot of men had gone just a little silly over women, and Stanley was only human!

Stella steeled herself to confront him when he came home. No other woman was going to steal her husband without a fight - especially a floozie called Florence, not if she could help it!

Then she heard the gate open, and the sound of his bike as he wheeled it along the path. The door opened and he stood there, smiling that old, mischievous smile of his.

'I've got something to tell you,' he said, putting an arm around her shoulders.

'About Florence?'

He removed his arm from around her shoulders, surprised by the question.

'How could you possibly know that?' he demanded, as he pulled out an envelope from his inside pocket.

'You told me,' she replied, 'in your sleep, I know all about Florence.'

'Damn!' he snorted indignantly. 'Of all the times to talk in my sleep.'

He handed her the envelope, and she withdrew two airline tickets to Florence, dated Saturday.

'Happy Anniversary,' he said as he kissed her. Then he added, 'I'm sorry that I spoiled the surprise by talking in my sleep, though.'

'You didn't spoil it,' Stella replied, with a catch in her voice, 'I thought Florence was a woman.'

Stanley took a step back.

'You surely didn't think I could fall for another woman, did you?'

'I didn't know what to think,' Stella sobbed. 'We've never had secrets before, and there you were, riding off on that bike of yours, telling me that you were going fishing - and your rod still in the house. Telling me that you had business to see to but not telling me what it was. What was I to think?'

Stanley put his arm back around her shoulders.

'I'm sorry I upset you, love, but I really couldn't fall for another woman. You know what they say, two's company... ?'

Drive Me

by

Jean M Warner

'How about a Fly Drive holiday in the States, darling?' my husband suggested.

He grinned at the stunned expression on my face as he flung some brochures on the table. I was used to most of his sudden surprises, but this time I knew that he was likely to misinterpret my reaction. After all, he'd probably never witnessed blind panic before. In a split second, my emotions plunged from delight to despair as the full implication of that word 'drive' registered in my mind.

Poor man! He had never been able to understand my intense dislike of driving. For me it was an unpleasant, but necessary duty; a penalty for enjoying all the other benefits of modern day living. So I drove only when I had to, rating it on a par with visiting the dentist or filling out a tax form. I was just a natural for the passenger seat.

Now, glumly I sat alongside him, determined not to let my phobia spoil his plans for the holiday of a lifetime. Oblivious to my mood, he got out some maps and happily began planning a route.

'Once we get used to the automatic hire car with its left hand drive,' he prattled on, 'we'll be able to cover a lot of ground. Pity about the fifty-five speed limit over there. Of course, we'll share the driving like we always do on long trips here.'

'Of course,' I echoed brightly.

It didn't seem fair that all the pleasure about the trip was already over for me. Carefree meant car free in my vocabulary! Under my breath I recited 'for better, for worse, 'til death us do part.' That set me wondering if my Will was in an accessible place. Friends or relatives might need to find it.

Next day at work, I casually asked my three female colleagues about their driving experiences abroad.

'Never done any on holiday,' the first retorted. 'We take our car over to the south of France every year, but my husband hogs all the driving to himself. I just sit there, bored to tears most of the time.'

I stared at her. What a gift of a man. I'd never met him, but incipient ideas of husband swapping seemed very plausible.

'It's terrible,' the second declared, shuffling piles of papers on her desk. 'We drove in Spain once. I hated it. Utter bedlam! Cars coming at you from all sides. And such hooting. A bull fight 'd be more peaceful.'

'Oh! Go on!' the third and youngest chided. 'I drove a good bit in the States when I went with my boyfriend a couple of years ago. It's dead easy! It only takes you a little while to get used to the car and then - zoom! You're off and away. Smashing cars they are too! Much better than ours.'

They then began talking about something else while I relapsed into silence.

From then on everything seemed to gang up against me. TV programmes featured American car chase films with sickening regularity. Newspapers displayed pictures and articles about accidents and driving disasters that I could well have done without. It all set me longing to have been born in the good old days of horse drawn transport. I even toyed with the idea of taking secret lessons on an automatic car before we set off, but discreet enquiries made me squash this plan. British models are different in design and it would only add to my confusion.

My husband never suspected the turmoil I was in, and I hoped fervently that he'd never find out. It certainly didn't help me much when he came home with the information that it was advisable to take out special insurance.

'There's a Hit and Run Insurance Protection policy, also an Uninsured Motorists Protection scheme,' he explained cheerfully one evening. 'The travel agent said that it's a two-in-one cover. As you can't be too careful, I've taken out a million dollar policy for us!'

It didn't feel like I thought it should. I went numb. Luckily, when we went to have our photos taken for the International Driving permit, I was not expected to smile.

'It's like a passport, darling,' my ever-knowledgeable husband told me. 'We only need to carry it for identification purposes. Apparently, the Americans have problems understanding our driving licenses. That's what the travel agent said, anyway.'

Resisting the temptation to suggest that he went away with his precious travel agent instead of me, I tried to focus my attention on what we needed to pack.

Departure day eventually dawned. As we drove down to the airport, my husband commented on the fact that he was glad I wasn't like some people he knew.

'Oh! Just what do you mean by that?' I asked, gazing wistfully, probably for the last time, at the familiar landmarks we were passing.

'Well, some people are afraid of flying. Never could understand them. It's far safer than driving a car.'

That was the moment I very nearly hit him!

Our long flight was most enjoyable. I was determined to savour at least this experience to the full. When the pilot announced that we were over land, I peered through the tiny window to get my first glimpse of what lay below. My battlefield was stretched out beneath me. It all looked very big. There were long, straight, unbelievably empty roads. Next, the little clusters of houses gave way to civilisation in the form of towns and cities. Blue swimming pools glinted in the sunlight. As the plane began its descent, I could see cars moving like highly polished, busy insects. Now was the time to sit back and think of England! An all too familiar voice broke my trance.

'I'm glad we decided to spend our first night at one of the airport hotels,' he purred contentedly. 'It'll give us the chance to adjust to the time change. They will take us to pick up the car tomorrow.'

We got a warm and friendly welcome at the hotel and were shown into our spacious room. In spite of the comfort of the king-size bed, I did not sleep very well. I had too much on my mind.

Next morning, we arrived at the car rental depot and filled in all the necessary forms. The keys to our four door, air conditioned model were handed over. Happiness fairly oozed from my partner, as he listened to all the instructions and pocketed the documents. In total silence we drove back to the hotel. His was that of utter bliss. Mine has not yet been satisfactorily categorised. Back in the parking lot he drew up in one of the many empty bays.

'You try it out now, darling!'

Reluctantly, I settled myself into the driving seat and tried to concentrate on what we had been told.

'Right,' he beamed, 'have a go on your own while I settle up and get our luggage.'

Then he left me alone with my mechanical foe.

After a moment, I slid my hands appreciatively over the upholstery. It really was a beautiful car. Everything about it was designed for comfort. Four people would have had ample leg room front and back. I felt as if I was sitting in an arm chair. But then everything here seemed so well planned. Town and cities had been designed specifically for the car. They hadn't had to adapt to it as we had done in our tiny, crowded island. I thought of our congested roads, and lack of parking space. There were few controls in front of me and I was pleased that there was no clutch to worry about. Gears were automatic. One lever with clear markings was all there was alongside the steering wheel. Gently, I took hold of it. Moving its position from neutral into drive, I released the handbrake. The great car obediently moved forward. With growing surprise, I discovered that the steering wheel responded to the lightest touch. Featherlight pressure also activated the brakes. Now I decided to make a tour all round the vast expanse of the hotel's parking lot. Then I reversed into a space. Thrilled with the scale of my accomplishment, I did a second tour and drew up at the hotel entrance just as my husband emerged through its doors.

'It's easy!' I announced in a voice of total disbelief, 'and I think I'll enjoy it!'

'But of course, dear!' He sounded surprised. 'That's why I planned this driving holiday especially for you!'

Dog Tired

by

Raymond Gridley

Would you spend the night with a strange dog on your bed?

Me neither, but there it was - one horizontal hound lying there on the bed made up for me! I tried everything from sweet talk to threats to get it to move but to no avail. The owners would have to be summoned from their slumber if I was going to get any sleep that night.

I knocked on the bedroom door of my hosts.

'Excuse me. Sorry to trouble you, but there's a big hound on my bed.'

Husband and wife exchanged knowing glances.

'Ah, yes. That'll be Dog. If he's claimed your bed then you've got problems.'

'You've got problems,' echoed spouse.

The three of us ventured into the bedroom to assess the situation. Dog - that was his name (due to an hereditary lack of creativity in the family) - was still lying there, legs outstretched. My initial diagnosis was canine catatonia. I based this on the observation that there was no discernible movement as my host prodded him with the spongy end of the floor mop.

'It sometimes works,' he explained feebly. Well it didn't this time. I immediately demanded proof that the object lying on my bed was in fact a living entity - capable of at least a few basic movements.

An indignant host then picked him up bodily, placed him on his paws and issued orders to castrate me. I can only assume that the thought of any physical activity other than breathing induced a state of apoplexy into Dog, for he promptly fell sideways and assumed his original position. I then instigated a discussion on the correct procedures for administering the last rites, but was assured that this would not be necessary and in any case the handle on the shovel was broken. The production of the family photo album showing Dog in various states of muscular activity in his younger days disproved my theory that he had about as much energy as an anaemic tortoise.

'Why can't we just chuck him off?' I enquired.

Husband and wife exchanged knowing glances.

'He protests.'

'Both ends,' added spouse. 'It's terrible sometimes - the noise! The mess! We've found it's best just to let... '

'Sleeping dogs lie,' I interjected.

'Yes quite.'

While we were pondering the next move one-who-should-have-been-in-bed appeared, clutching a teddy.

'I know how to get him off the bed,' she said teasingly.

'How? How?'

'You have to sing him that song he hates.'

'What song?' we replied in unison.

'Oh, I can't remember it - something to do with home.'

Well, we sang every song we could think of with the word home in it: Home on the Range, Home Cooking, Keep the Home Fires Burning, Hometown, Homeward Bound, Westering Home, Going Home, There's No Place Like Home, Back in Your Own Backyard (in desperation). Nothing worked and my accompanying songsters were slowly drifting off when I suddenly remembered one more song.

'Wait, I know one: Show Me The Way To Go Home!' OK so we tried it out and watched for a reaction.

The first indication came with a twitching of Dog's nose, then an irritable flapping of the ears. Suddenly the full force of the song had registered on Dog's consciousness and two bloodshot eyes sprang up from Dog's face. I don't know what the high jump record is for the canine world but I'm certain I witnessed a personal best from Dog. Fortunately the bedroom door was open, but I'm sure that an inch and a half of Columbian Pine would have been no match for the force behind Dog's departure from the room. A resounding cheer rang out from the quartet. We eventually found Dog ensconced under the kitchen table in a state of post-melodic shock. No matter, I had my bed back and could get a night's sleep. I bid goodnight to my hosts once again and returned to the bedroom. Well, I had to tidy the bed - Dog had certainly ruffled all the bedclothes up. The pillow seemed to be extra lumpy.

One minute later I was knocking on the bedroom of my hosts.

'Excuse me. Sorry to trouble you. I didn't know you had a cat. Do you happen to know any songs it doesn't like?'

Hotline

by

Guy Pearson

It was still and hot on this summer Sunday in the North Midlands countryside. The sort of day often prayed for when planning a party but, with all best laid plans; rarely granted. The champagne had just been put on ice when Hilary entered the library. The Crowthers called it that simply for want of a better description for the high-ceilinged room with its sombre dark panels and tall narrow windows. It faced east and got a little early sun in the summer. On the rare days like this the house and garden had shimmered in bright heat from early morning and the grave room made the ideal retreat for the pre-lunch gathering of some forty people. A fine setting for an anniversary to remember.

Hilary looked hot and flustered as she apologised to her guests for her absence. A slim woman on the edge of middle age and the ominous forties, her dark hair was carefully combed to hide the first traces of betraying grey. Her hair and large soft eyes were her best features. She made a striking figure in her multi-coloured dress as she fluttered from group to group like a visiting butterfly. She finally rested by the long table laden with ice buckets with their bottles thrusting like snowdrops eager to be noticed.

'Good heavens,' she said. She was more composed now as she turned to accept a glass. 'What must you all think of us. Tom will be down in a moment. He's just waiting to take an important 'phone call.' Hilary turned to the waiter behind the table. 'Please see that everyone is served. My husband will be down directly.' She turned to the assembled guests and the conversation, temporarily lulled, started up again as the filled glasses were handed round. No one noticed as Hilary disappeared again.

The sun had just slanted into the room turning it into a magic of golds and reds. Glasses were refilled several times before Hilary re-appeared. This time there was no colour in her face and she appeared unnaturally calm. Her voice, though quiet, had a compelling coldness that stilled the buzz of conversation.

'Tom won't be coming down.' She said.

She paused for a moment as if she was trying to find the right words. Her voice tailed off to a whisper. 'I think he's dead.'

27

Hilary's stark statement had more effect than a flood of tears or an outbreak of female hysteria. There followed a moment of stunned silence then the inevitable questions.

'When, How, Why.'

They flowed around Hilary as she sat silently slumped in a chair by the glass laden table.

Jack Milton came over to the crumpled figure and put his arm around her shoulder. 'I'll go up.' He said simply.

Jack was the family doctor and had known Hilary since childhood. Since her marriage he had also become a close friend of Tom and was visibly shaken by the news but he took his leave of Hilary and made his way upstairs. Some of Hilary's closest friends clustered round her making sympathetic mutterings while others drifted out into the garden in awkward silence.

Hilary came from good class farming stock that had known better times. Her only real adventure with the opposite sex had been in her early twenties but this first fling had ended in pure disaster. It had culminated in an abortion as an alternative to single parenthood. The whole thing had been concealed from the local community by a long holiday abroad. No one outside her own family knew the full story and on her return she threw out a defence mechanism to prevent a repeat mistake. No one had got through it until she met Tom. That was at a political fund raising function in the nearby town. Hilary's defences were breached in the first few minutes and they were married within weeks.

Tom was a newcomer to the district. He had come up from the concrete wastelands of East London just as the property boom was nearing its peak. In a few short years he had used his second sight for a property bargain to good effect. From a small time builder he had progressed, through a series of shrewd purchases and renovations into a not-so-small developer. His final coup was when a site he had held only two years netted a small fortune when sold for a supermarket development. He banked his last fat cheque and headed North where his capital would buy more. Within weeks he had purchased a rambling manor house with acres he didn't believe still existed. Labour was plentiful and in a few months he had the old place back on its feet. Then he met Hilary. She was the jewel he sought and the old house was just the right setting.

The couple were popular in the area. Hilary had a wide circle of friends into which Tom was readily accepted. His cropped brown hair was already greying at the edges but his figure kept the lean, wiry look of an active man. His open look and bluff manner was readily appreciated by the Northerners and the marriage looked as solid as the stone outcrops that surrounded their home. But like many stones, there had to be a flaw somewhere.

The flaw in this marriage was children, or rather the lack of them. Tom wanted... Hilary did not. And, being a sensible girl now, she had the final say.

The dissent over a family was not the only secret that no one knew abut. For years they kept the guise of a perfect couple and their ages was good reason for the lack of offspring.

What no one knew, least of all Tom, was that Hilary had taken a lover. He had been a member of her intimate circle for some years before Tom appeared on the scene. Then, like her first lover, he had uprooted and taken off for the 'golden triangle' in the South East. His flair for electronics was his ticket to a progressive firm holding large Government contracts in electronic and surveillance systems. Hilary knew little of this and cared less. Letters from Alan gradually petered out until that fateful day a year ago. Alan had progressed to Technical Director when the bubble burst.

Government contracts dried up and the firm sank without trace. Alan returned to his roots where he met Hilary again on one of her shopping forays in the County town. They met and re-met over the following weeks. Hilary wasn't in love with Alan but she was no longer in love with Tom either. She was still looking for something else. Something she failed to find in her first mad affair. Perhaps she was merely trying to break free from the routine in which she was now trapped. It was then that the bizarre plot was hatched.

Tom had the house, the money, the lot. Everything was in his name and she could see it staying that way... With Tom's money she could escape before it was too late. A few months earlier Tom had effected a very substantial insurance which would bring his estate to nearly two million pounds. This, together with the pure excitement of the plan itself, drove her on. Alan, also at the crossroads, was swept up in the mad idea. It took him some time to perfect the device that would arrange that most elusive thing... the perfect murder.

The means to achieve this was Alan's adaption of a miniature stun device. It could be fitted in seconds to the earpiece of a standard telephone receiver. Lifting the handset triggered the device giving the person holding it a fatal shock. The effect lasted only a few seconds after which the instrument was harmless. The device could then be removed leaving no trace of its presence. All that was needed was the perfect timing for the call.

The wedding anniversary was selected as the day for the fateful call. They had the motive, the opportunity and the method. This was ideal with dozens of guests for alibis.

The hum of low conversation returned to Hilary as she sat in silence in the chair. She knew that Jack Milton would be down in a moment. She had never socialised with him very much but the Doctor had struck up a friendship with Tom from the very start. They shared a common interest in golf and fish. Of these, fish came first with Tom. He had them everywhere, from the large very expensive carp in the outside pool to the huge tank of tropicals he insisted on keeping in the bedroom. The large unit was kept on a specially constructed base that held the telephone and some indoor plants.

The Doctor would find Tom looking much the same in death as in life... solid and uninteresting. No spectacular pool of blood, no signs of injury, no outward signs of cause at all. The actual instrument of cause had been removed. Hilary had seen to that. It had taken only seconds to remove that from the handset lying beside the tank. It had been a little un-nerving stretching over the fallen body to remove the evidence.

Alan had made the call exactly on time, just ten minutes after her first visit to the bedroom. A pretext had sent Tom from the room long enough to fit the device.

Her second visit removed it. Dr Milton would find nothing wrong. His diagnosis would be the high-flyers arch enemy... a heart attack.

The Doctor returned down the stairs and approached her slowly as she looked up. He was grave of face and manner.

'I'm so sorry Hilary,' he said softly. 'I am afraid that Tom is, indeed, dead.' He paused for a moment. 'I cannot say the exact cause.' He held out his hands to Hilary who took them silently.

The guests melted discreetly into the garden and the Doctor turned away for a moment. Then he turned to Hilary again, his face creased in a puzzled frown.

'There's one thing I don't understand,' Milton continued. 'Nothing to do with Tom, of course, but all his fish decided to die at the same time.' He rubbed his chin as he muttered, almost to himself, 'Most odd, most odd.'

Hilary wasn't listening. She suddenly realised that Tom must have dropped the 'phone, still 'live' for a few seconds, by the tropical tank. That was long enough to kill all the sensitive occupants. In her hurry to remove the device she had not noticed that they, like Tom, were still and lifeless.

Friendships

by

Susan Knight

'Why don't you ring him up and ask him out?'

My best friend, Laura, was madly in lust with her ex, Zac. She went out with him for a couple of months a while back, and hadn't seen or mentioned him since, until she bumped into him two weeks ago on the bus, after school. All I had heard about since was Zac, Zac, and more Zac. Even though I had been appointed official matchmaker, I fancied him for myself. If Laura wasn't my best friend, maybe things would have been different.

'Won't you ring him for me?' Laura begged.

'Chicken!'

'Am not! It's just, well, what if he turns me down?'

'Then it's his loss, not yours.'

I secretly hoped that he would turn her down. I hated myself for wanting Zac to hurt her, but I couldn't help my feelings for him and they were driving me mad.

That night I sat up at home, desperately trying to finish some work that had to be given in the next day but all I could think about was Zac. I was abruptly interrupted by the telephone - it was Laura.

'Guess who just rang me?'

'Who?' I asked, trying to sound vaguely interested.

'Zac!' she said, dreamily.

'What did he want?' I asked sharply, dreading the answer.

'He's asked me out to the club tomorrow night, why don't we make it the four of us?'

'Me and who?' I asked distantly.

'Dave, of course, silly!'

Dave was my boyfriend. I finished the call quickly, trying to hold back the tears. How could Zac ask her out? I was sure he wasn't interested in her.

I wasn't looking forward to the next night either. I'm not into double dating, and a night with Dave was bad enough (he was starting to annoy me), but watching Laura and Zac dribbling all over each other wasn't exactly my idea of fun either.

31

The evening actually wasn't that bad. We went to the nightclub, and I got a bit drunk. I made it pretty clear about my feeling towards both Dave and Zac, and I thought Zac seemed pretty interested. But the evening ended in a massive row between me and Laura who accused me of trying to crack onto Zac.

I rang Laura the next day, to apologise, blaming the booze, and I told her that I only liked Zac as a friend. She said she believed me and she was sorry for accusing me.

Later that day I went round to her house on my way to Dave's. She was out... with Zac.

I apologised to Dave and made up some story about him moving too fast and that I wasn't ready for that sort of commitment yet (at least, not with him). He believed me and I made a mental note not to go out with such a loser again. In the darkness on the way home I met Zac.

'Hi! Where's Laura?' I asked trying to sound casual.

'She had to go.'

I was pleased, in a nasty sort of way.

'Do you remember last night?' he enquired.

'Yes it was good.'

I was really embarrassed and I kept wishing I hadn't drunk so much.

'I didn't know you felt that way, about me, I mean.'

'Oh,' I replied. What could I say? I felt uncomfortable.

'Would you like to go out with me?' he asked.

It was so out of the blue, I couldn't believe it.

'Yes, I'd love to - but it would have to be our secret, you wouldn't tell Laura, would you?'

'She is your best friend.'

I didn't need reminding - she was my only friend and I couldn't really afford to lose her, even for Zac.

'What she won't know can't hurt her, can it?'

Suddenly Laura stepped out of the darkness. I realised Zac had lied, she had been there all the time, and I had fallen into their trap. She took Zac's hand and I couldn't bear to watch.

'Some friend you are,' she screamed as they walked away.

I called after her, 'Laura, wait, I can explain, I'm sorry Laura...'

But they had gone, leaving me alone... with the darkness.

The Stroke

by

Elaine Kempton

The stroke had left Louisa half blind, partially paralysed and totally confused. It was out of the question for her to continue living alone in the rambling old house on the Cornish coast. She was brought to London by her distraught daughter Caroline, who loved her dearly and was determined to look after her. The spare bedroom of the house where Caroline and her husband Geoff lived became Louisa's home. Caroline gave up her job and stayed with her mother, caring for her with total devotion. For several weeks Louisa was completely bedridden. She had to be fed and washed and was seemingly oblivious to what was happening around her. For this Caroline was grateful. She was ashamed of the disgust that she felt dealing with her mother's incontinence, she hated the huge pads, like grotesque sanitary towels, that she had to place between Louisa's legs. She loathed herself because changing the soiled pads made her stomach heave. She was glad that her mother was unaware of this, her own disgust was hard enough for her to cope with, the distress Louisa would have felt had she been aware of her own lack of dignity and privacy would have been too much for her. She had always been proud and independent, rarely asking for help and insisting on keeping on the large house when her husband had died ten years previously. She had been a familiar figure in the village, driving herself around, content to spend her old age in her beloved Cornwall. The stroke had been sudden, there had been nothing to prepare Caroline for the complete change in her mother. She and Geoff had spent Easter with Louisa in the West Country, there had been no sign that anything was wrong. It had been a pleasant stay, Louisa was her usual busy, self-reliant self, gardening, baking, entertaining them with amusing anecdotes of village life. She had driven them through the winding lanes and dragged them on long walks across the cliffs. When they had left to return to London she had packed them a picnic for on the way home and given Caroline strict instructions to telephone her when they arrived back so that she would know they were safe. The next time Caroline had seen her mother was three weeks later. She was lying in a hospital bed, semi-comatose, attached to a drip, her face distorted. Her life was over but her heart was still beating.

33

Gradually Louisa had improved. She was able to take herself to the toilet, shuffling awkwardly from her room to the bathroom, making Caroline wait outside until she had finished, then allowing her to help her back to bed. Mercifully she seemed to have no memory of the weeks of having to be changed and washed like a baby. She no longer stayed in bed all the time, she fed herself and slowly became more alert and aware. She regained some of the use of her arms and legs. Her sight however did not improve, everything remained misty and out of focus. For Louisa this was the ultimate torment, she could no longer read. She loved books with a passion and had spent many hours reading. She didn't want talking books or cassettes, she wanted to sit with a book of her choice and read it as and when she pleased. As her mind cleared she realised the enormity of what had happened to her. She would watch Caroline with dark, resentful eyes, their roles becoming reversed. As a sick child will sometimes become angry with it's mother for being unable to make it better, Louisa behaved so badly towards Caroline that she would reduce her to tears several times a day. Sometimes she wouldn't speak at all except to demand to be taken home, back to her own house. Caroline would tell her that it was impossible, explain why it was impossible but Louisa didn't seem to hear.

Caroline tried her best to make life pleasant for her mother. She spent hours in the kitchen preparing dishes from The Invalid Cook Book. She acquired a wheelchair and tried to tempt her with offers of outings to Kew Gardens or Hampton Court. Geoff hired a van and drove to Cornwall, bringing back some of Louisa's smaller pieces of furniture, her plants and her ornaments, so that she could have her own familiar things in her room. The house was in the hands of a reputable estate agent but in an already depressed market the chances of a quick sale were almost nil. The sale of the house would release enough money for Caroline and her husband to buy a larger house more suited to Louisa's needs. Caroline was sure that, given time, her mother would come to terms with things and they would all be able to make the best of a dreadful situation.

Louisa knew that she would never come to terms with the way that her life had become. She knew that she was making her daughter's life a misery but she couldn't stop. She was locked in her own despair, caught in the nightmare that her existence now was. She could no longer do any of the things that had given her pleasure. She hated the disruption that she had brought to Caroline and Geoff's life. She loved them both. Caroline was her only child and they had always been close. Over the years Geoff had become like her own child too. She wanted happiness for them both. They had chosen not to have children of their

34

own yet they were now tied by her. She knew that she couldn't be left alone, she needed help with the most simple of tasks.

The rage and frustration she felt at her own useless body left her weak. Why wouldn't her arms work properly? Why wouldn't her legs just move like they were supposed to, like they always had? They looked like her limbs but they wouldn't do what she willed them to do, what they were meant to. Even when, slowly and painfully, she could move about she couldn't see clearly enough to be able to dress herself or put her hair up or powder her face. Caroline had brought her a large television but all she could see were nebulous shapes on the screen. She wanted to rub and rub her eyes until the mists cleared, but even if her useless arms would have let her she knew that the mists were never ever going to clear. She was always going to be partially sighted and she couldn't bear it. The rage and terror that she felt made normal behaviour impossible. She knew that she should feel gratitude to Caroline and Geoff, she shuddered when she thought of how much worse things would have been had they abandoned her to the System. Some anonymous ward in a geriatric hospital or Old People's Home. She wished that the stroke had killed her instead of leaving her like this. Much as she longed for death she was afraid of the act of dying. Then she understood that she was afraid because she didn't really want to die, she wanted her life back. Memories of the person that she used to be tortured her, she mourned for her dead self, for the Louisa who had gone. She perceived her existence now as a kind of half way house, Louisa May Hardwick was dead, a useless, embittered creature inhabited her body, which could not be buried. So she remained, somewhere between living and dying, cheated of her life, denied the dignity of death. There was no respite, nothing she could do to alleviate her misery and so she inflicted it on the person that she loved the most. Some nights she could dream that she was whole again, at home in Cornwall. Tending her garden, the air heavy with the scent of honeysuckle, the sun shining on her as she sat by the pond reading or sewing or writing letters. She would wake reluctantly, struggling to return to her dream and her past, knowing the harsh reality of the coming day. Her pillow would be wet with tears and she would have to try to turn it over so that Caroline wouldn't know.

Caroline was acutely aware of her mother's distress but was powerless to do anything. Geoff suffered for his wife and also for Louisa, of whom he was deeply fond. They were all trapped in their own misery and there seemed no way out. Louisa had accused them of trying to cheat her and sell her property for their own selfish gain and so they had taken the house off the market and closed it up.

35

The loss of Caroline's income was becoming apparent, she desperately missed her work and her colleagues. She would look at her mother, staring silently into space and she would know her inner torment. Her heart ached for her and also for herself. It was as if she had lost her mother and she felt so alone without her. Louisa had always been there for her. She had advised her, comforted her and guided her all of her life and the void that was left was painful to bear. She remembered her childhood and how patient and kind her mother had always been. She had been someone real and solid during all the traumas of adolescence and when Caroline had grown up, left home, travelled and finally settled with Geoff her mother had been her friend and her mentor. When her father had died, even though Caroline had been a grown woman, Louisa had held and comforted her and they had survived. In a strange, obscure way, as she struggled to care for and cope with her mother, she missed her mother.

As Christmas approached Louisa seemed to sink deeper into despair. She hardly ate, she seldom spoke except to complain, she didn't want to get out of bed and yet she rarely seemed to sleep. The doctor prescribed sleeping pills and tranquillisers. Caroline half-heartedly decorated the house, the Christmas tree, shimmering with lights and baubles seemed a travesty. But she persevered, hoping, praying that maybe Louisa may glean some tiny bit of pleasure from the festive season. Who knew what miracles Christmas could bring? In the week leading up to the 25th of December she would give Louisa her breakfast and her pills, leave her a flask of coffee and a sandwich and venture to the shops. Her shopping would be rushed, she hated to leave her mother alone and yet when she returned, Louisa would still be sitting as she had left her, the sandwich uneaten, the thermos flask still full. She would chat to her, show her what she had brought. There would be little, if any response.

On Christmas Eve Caroline overslept. She was angry, she had so much to do that day. She rushed around, Louisa refused to eat her breakfast and so she left her with just a cup of milky coffee and her pills. The shops were crowded with smiling, bustling people and Caroline remembered happier years when she too had smiled and hurried around, complaining but secretly loving all the activity.

As a last minute gift, with little hope of appreciation, she bought Louisa a tape of traditional Christmas carols to go with the many little presents she had bought her and then she went home. She unpacked her shopping, turned on the oven to bake mince pies and made a pot of tea to take up for her and Louisa to drink. While the tea brewed she unplugged the radio cassette, inserted the tape of Christmas carols ready to play and took the whole lot on a tray up to Louisa's room.

She knew as soon as she opened the door that there was something wrong. Louisa was lying on the bed, apparently asleep, the bottle of tranquillisers empty beside the coffee cup. Caroline stood and took in the scene! She must have forgotten to screw the cap back on the bottle of pills, she'd been in such a hurry. Quite calmly she went over to her mother and tried to wake her, knowing it was useless. Louisa's breathing was shallow, her eyelids flickered and then her eyes opened wide and met Caroline's and in that moment all the love that she had been unable to show her daughter for so long shone through. Caroline held her hand and stroked her hair.

'It's okay Mum, you'll be alright, I'm going to phone an ambulance,' she whispered gently.

Louisa gripped her hand, surprising Caroline with the strength of her hold. Her voice was barely audible, 'Don't darling, please don't.' And so she didn't. She plugged in the tape player, 'Silent Night, Holy Night' filled the room and they stayed quietly together. Mother and daughter, locked in love. When Louisa wasn't breathing anymore Caroline went downstairs and telephoned for an ambulance.

Naked Reader

by

Alan Phillips

After the phone call from Nicola the prospect of being a model turned over in Faine's mind. For the whole weekend she was preoccupied with the idea of pos-ing naked. She wouldn't say anything to Oscar yet perhaps she would confide in Cecile. Maybe it would go off well. She still had a good figure.

On the Sunday afternoon she sunbathed in the garden. Through the French windows she could see her daughter.

'Darling,' she called, 'would you come and cream my back.'

Cecile came out, took the tube of Ambre Solaire and commenced to smooth cream over Faine's back and shoulders.

'That's lovely,' Faine said. 'You have such a gentle touch. Its so soothing to have someone apply it, especially between the shoulders, where it's hard to reach.'

Cecile said, 'I'll do you all over. You have a nice figure, you know. You could have been a model. How would you have liked that? All swishy and swanky on the catwalk.'

'It might be better than word processing.' Faine's voice was day-dreamy under the massage.

'But you really have got a nice figure, Mummy. Lucky you have; your taste in bikinis is minimal. They say it's beneficial between the scapulas because that's where the nerve centres are.'

'It's so soothing - I feel like a stroked cat - I could start purring - prrrrr.' Faine laughed.

'It's because it smooths out all those jangled nerves and muscles and sinews, Cecile said. 'There, you lovely near-naked thing. I have to leave you now.'

'Thank you for your ministrations.'

'You're welcome sweetie.' Cecile kissed Faine's back and went into the house.

She would have preferred to have been nude. They had tried it on the beach at Cap d'Agde where Oscar had gone on the beach with them, without himself stripping. She would say nothing about the posing she had accepted for

Monday evening. She felt heady fear and anticipation - but was set on going through with it.

When the time came she found that her jitters had been unwarranted. She walked out and asked what kind of pose they would like, reclining, seated or standing. And tutor and students were kind and appreciative. The lady tutor asked frequently if she wanted a rest, and when the time was up said she would be in touch with regard to further engagements. They all remarked on how still the new model was. Some models, they said, wanted to move or have a rest every five minutes. At home she said nothing at first, but in the end conveyed the news almost casually, as they sat at supper next evening.

'I have something to tell you both.' She said it with smile, as if to make light of it. 'I've found myself a new occupation. I've posed as a life model, and they think I'm very good.'

Oscar and Cecile looked at her.

'A life model,' Oscar queried. 'What's that? Are they the ones that model clothes?'

Faine could see her daughter's smile and she laughed slightly. 'No,' she said. 'Life models pose for artists.'

'What?' Oscar said. 'Without anything on you mean?'

'Yes,' Faine said simply.

'Naked?'

'Yes.'

'How did you get a start in this, Mummy?' Cecile sounded rather taken by the new development. Her voice had a tinge of envy.

'Well,' Faine smiled. 'I knew Nicola was a part-time model. She'd told me about it and I once let slip a remark that I fancied trying it myself. I'd read a library book about models and we were talking about it. Nicola had completely overlooked that Monday was parents evening at the school and she thought Lucy would be disappointed if she didn't go. So she asked me to take her place.'

Oscar seemed to be seeking words. Faine felt she'd throw in a light touch.

'I thought it would make a change from word processing - give the brain cells a rest.'

Oscar exploded, 'Well - I think it's disgraceful. A woman of your age, displaying herself naked in public.'

Faine tried reasoning.

'But, look, you accept that the figure should be portrayed in works of art. Therefore models, and sometimes nude models, are essential to the artist. Michelangelo and Leonardo used nude models. Therefore it cannot be wrong for people to pose in the nude - the Sistine Chapel is covered with Michelangelo's nudes. So if we accept that nude models are indispensable to great art it cannot be wrong in any way for somebody to pose in the nude. All I can suggest is that we agree to differ.'

She was due to read at mass the next Saturday evening. When she went up on the sanctuary she could see one of the students from the life class. A parishioner knew about her new occupation! Suppose it got all around the parish - everything always did. But she wasn't going to be put down by a lot of gossips. Then another voice said: You are being uncharitable. You are projecting your unworthy suspicions onto innocent people. You have an unconquerable desire to display yourself near-naked in your own garden, naked at Cap d'Agde, and naked in front of a roomful of people. And you are chairperson of a parish committee; how will you face them in future?

The bell tinkled and priest and servers clustered around the sacristy door. She made an effort, said a short prayer, and walked to the lectern. She delivered her opening lines.

'We celebrate the mass for the thirteenth Sunday of the year.' She paused a few moments, established some eye-contact. She could feel the eyes on her. She had been complimented for her reading. She could see the young art-class man near the front. She knew she had the knack of holding an audience. How would it affect her when they got to know?

'Let us say together the entrance antiphon.' Her delivery of the words commenced. 'All nations, clap your hands. Shout with a voice of joy to God.'

Amazing how we can feel things - the responsiveness of an audience. She had felt it with the eyes in the life class on her. Perhaps it was the same with paintings - some could receive and some not. The eyes of the young artist were on her. What could he be making of it! She would get through it somehow, turn tension into performance.

Faine retired to her side pew as servers and priest swept up onto the altar. The celebrant turned to greet his audience:

'We are gathered here in the presence of Christ. The second reading for today tells us how we are to love one another. The more we love the more we will join together our whole community.'

After the Gloria, Faine moved out to give the main readings. She put all else aside and gave her best to the first reading. When she went into the responsorial psalm she could feel them responding, clear and beautiful and un-mistakable. The young artist was joining in. She thought of how she could hold an audience with her voice and her body. The studio she had posed in was not far from the church. Suppose - just suppose. She delivered the second reading from Saint Paul to the Galations... 'being called to know liberty... be careful in case liberty should provide an opening for self indulgence... serve one another in works of love...' Well, it was a form of love, an expression of it, to give one-self ... to offer one's body as a model... to offer one's voice in reading.

The priest read the gospel and delivered a charming short sermon about it being important to love the body as guest chamber of the soul.

What would she do if it got around? Leave the country! But she steeled her-self to come out and read the bidding prayers and she knew a certain relief when her reading was finished and she could descend from the sanctuary.

She remained with head bowed until it was time to offer a hand in the sign of peace and she offered it to those around her, including the young artist, ex-changing a 'Peace be with you.'

At the end she went to light a candle. As she turned from murmuring a prayer she saw the young man approaching.

'May I congratulate you on your two wonderful talents.'

'Thank you,' Faine said with a diffident smile.

'You read so well, you make people want to listen. And as a model you're fabulous. You remain so still - and you have the quality of inspiring people to draw you, to create something fresh and new.'

As they left the church the young man turned to her and said, 'I've done modelling myself but I'm not in your class. I wonder - er - are you willing to accept private engagements?'

Man Down Under

by

Molly Nixon

'I've had so many experiences since I came out here, mate. Maybe I'm bound to, travelling the outback like I do. Me and my old jalopy have done some miles. Work when I feel like it, eat when I can.

Aussies will share anything if you do a bit of work for them. They're supposed to hate Poms, but don't you believe it, mate. No one's ever given me a roasting. They like to take the mickey but it's all good natured. Bit of prejudice on the part of youngsters though. It's all this unemployment: Aussie kids don't like Poms having jobs they think should be theirs. I don't have any trouble because I'm only a casual.

Wouldn't change this life for anything, mate. Wouldn't go back to England: my missus couldn't trace me here. I'm on the move all the time. Even tried my hand at sheep shearing and made a few dollars that way.

My old jalopy is tied here and there with bits of rope. Sometimes she has to be coaxed, or kicked when she won't budge, but there's plenty of life in her yet, at least I hope so.

Funny thing happened a few weeks back. I was driving over the dust track on my way to Wallabonga. Dry as hell! Late afternoon, but still smelt as if the earth was scorching. Wanted to make Wallabonga before dark, or I'd have laid up somewhere. Suddenly saw a shack shimmering in the heat. Thought at first it was imagination. My eyes play funny tricks in this heat. Sure enough, it was a small wooden house. Looked like a white man's place. Hadn't seen a white face in days. Lots of abbos though and I get on well enough with them.

Decided to stop at the shack. Always made welcome and given food and drink. Sometimes I stay a few days to help out. Even invited to a bit on the side if there are any dames about. Oh, boy! The stories I could tell if I'd a mind. I like to love 'em and leave 'em, no questions asked and no comebacks.

Well mate, I parked the old crate outside the front of the shack and swaggered up to the door. Couldn't understand why no-one came out to greet me. Usually they're out before I get near the front door, with a welcome.

House wasn't a bad old place. Could do with a lick of paint. Someone had put up a rough fence all round it and a couple of goats were tethered under a sagging lean-to.

No-one seemed to be home though. Nothing round the back. No-one anywhere. Bit scary. Settled in the porch to wait. God, it was hot! Had a little doze. Been travelling since sun-up with only a small break midday.

After a bit, thought I could smell burning so went in the shack to investigate. Blinds were down and the house was real cool. In the outhouse I found a coffee pot on the stove boiled dry and hissing and sizzling. Turned off the heat. The coffee pot had had it. Table was laid for two. Rum do! Began to look over my shoulder, I can tell you.

You could tell a woman lived there. All neat and tidy. Reminded me of how my missus used to spit and polish back home before we had a real humdinger and I cleared out. Best thing I ever did in my life, mate.

Sorted the coffee pot out and settled down again to wait - this time in the rocker, but no one came. Something weird here. Decided to make Wallabonga before dark.

Just trying to start the old jalopy when I heard a noise getting louder and louder and a van came bumping and screeching along the dust track, sending up showers of dirt that nearly choked me. Pulled up with a bang and a big, beefy man, farmer type, practically fell out of it.

'Who're you?' he barked. 'Where's my wife?' He must have thought I had her in my old car from the way he acted.

'I've been here since mid-afternoon and I've not seen anyone,' said I. 'I'd just decided to make Wallabonga and bed down there.'

'Oh, no, you don't,' he bawled, grabbing me by the arm and frog-marching me into the shack, which was so dim by now it was difficult to see anything.

'I've not seen your missus, honest to God. I've been travelling the bush for days and you're the first white person I've seen in a week.'

'Where the hell is she then? She was here when I left this morning and if you've been up to any monkey business I'll kill you.' Thought he was going to do it there and then, he was in such a rage. I was real scared. I can tell you.

Took a long time to calm him down and then we started searching. He kept me in front of him all the time. Still thought I'd done away with his old woman.

Where do you think we found the old girl after what seemed like hours of searching? Down the ruddy well, mate. Yes, she'd fallen down the well out back. Not much water in it or she'd have drowned, that's for sure. I offered to go to Wallabonga for help, but he wasn't having that. Seemed convinced I'd chucked her in, but luckily he needed help to get her out. We managed it between us. Don't know how she survived. She was alive all right. Must have been a tough old bird. She had concussion and was bashed about a bit, but we managed to get her comfy in bed.

That old man was still suspicious of me until the woman was able to tell him her story. She said she'd never set eyes on me before and all she could remember was she was looking down the well when she would swear she felt a bump on her backside. She couldn't account for it unless one of the goats had got loose. Goats were still chained up when I checked!

The old man asked me to stay over while she was laid up to keep an eye on things when he had to be away from the shack.

Well, mate, that old bird turned out to be quite a dish, nice and plump and just how I like 'em. She had masses of lovely golden hair, which she always let down when the old man was out of the way - and her eyes. Real 'come-hither' they were. Couldn't wait to get her to bed and when I did I wondered how she survived without someone like me around.

Not long before we were shacked up every time her husband went off for the day. Didn't get much work done then. I think he was getting suspicious from the dirty looks he kept giving me and the way he would suddenly appear when he wasn't expected home for hours.

Funny thing though, that old man went missing. Didn't come home for a couple of nights and I began to worry. Not so my bird. She reckoned he often stayed away for days on end, but I didn't like it. She was mad with me when I decided to go over to Wallabonga and see what the police thought of his disappearance.

They came over the next day, sniffing and searching around and asking questions. Where do you think they found him mate? Down the ruddy well, yes down the same ruddy well she had fallen into. Guess what I think? I think she'd upped him over with a bump on his backside when he was checking the water level. He was a goner all right when they pulled him out.

My bird told the police it must have been one of the goats, but those goats had never been off their chains.

I'm not daft. I hightailed it out of there before the plump bird got fed up with me. Everything is said to come in threes and I'm not one for taking chances.

She called me all sorts of names when she knew I was off, lots I'd never heard before. Well, I've not been in this country all that long and I'll probably extend my vocabulary in time.

44

A Flash in The Pan

by

Barrie Crowther

Jim Crowther opened his eyes and looked at the dappled light dancing on the ceiling, as it filtered through the trees outside his bedroom window.

He lay there in quiet contentment gathering his wits, trying to recall what day it was. With a start he remembered it was Saturday. A glance at his alarm clock showed 7am. Time to move. With a bound he shot out of bed and promptly upset a glass of water over his slippers. Opening the cornflakes packet, the contents of which ended up all over the floor. He started to plan his day.

The telephone rang in the office of 'Help the Aged', a volunteer group set up to help the elderly. Tom Stead picked up the phone.

'Good morning, 'Help the Aged, Halifax',' he said.

'This is the district nurse for Warely area,' came the pleasant voice in his ear.

'How can we help?' replied Tom.

'A patient of mine and her husband need your help. They live in an isolated cottage on Wainstalls Moor. They are having trouble with their electrical wiring, lights going off and on, that sort of thing. They don't complain but on their pension they can't afford an electrician.'

'Say no more,' said Tom. 'We have a standby sparkie. Just give me their name and address.'

Tom knew Jim Crowther well, or, as he was known by his pals as Flash. He got this nickname because as an apprentice electrician of 17, he left a spanner down the back of a circuit breaker they had just repaired. When the breaker was turned on the biggest flash ever seen in that factory was reported.

'Is that you, Flash? Now listen and write this down. A Mr and Mrs Barraclough of Delph Top, Moor Cottage, Wainstalls, need your help so get out there as soon as pos'. It's marked on your map.'

Flash duly arrived at Moor Cottage. It was like a scene from 'Wuthering Heights', in fact the Brontes used to live not so many miles over the moor to the north.

As he opened the door of his beat up old Transit van, he shivered in the freezing cold wind and this was summer!

45

As he was about to knock on the massive oak door, it was opened with such a creaking of hinges, he half expected Herman Munster to greet him. Instead a little old man with white hair, wearing a baggy cardigan with bony elbows sticking through holes in the sleeves.

'Come in, lad,' said Mr Barraclough. Flash followed him into the front room. Mrs Barraclough sat in an armchair, the white bandage on her leg contrasting sharply with the black velvet material of the upholstery.

'Glad to see you, lad. Would you like a cup of tea and a slice of home-made cake?'

'No thanks, Mrs Barraclough.'

'Call me Meg, everybody does.'

'Okay, I'm Flash.' The old couple looked at each other and laughed.

'As long as you're not Jumping Jack Flash,' said Meg and laughed again. The joke was lost on Jim.

'Right to business!' said the old man. 'When we switch the lights on they keep going off again.'

Flash said, 'Right. I'll check your fuse box and wiring.' The fuses seemed okay so he meggered the wiring. A megger is a small hand cranked generator, worked by turning the handle and then reading the meter scale. The wiring insulation was fine and Flash was thinking of the next move when the handle of the meggar started to turn in the opposite direction. 'That's strange,' he thought. He quickly gave it six rotations forward and released it. The handle immediately turned six rotations back the other way.

'What's up lad? You look fair flummoxed,' said Mr Barraclough.

'Oh oh it's nothing,' said Flash. 'I'll soon mend it.' He next tested the voltage: 240 volts as it should be. Then the thought struck him. It had to be a dicky switch. He fitted a new wall switch, left on the light and said to Meg, 'Right I'm ready for that cuppa now.'

The light had only been on five minutes when it went out. Flash with his cup half way to his mouth stopped.

'Hell fire jack!' he swore under his breath. Flash took a drink of tea.

'Do you think it's anything to do with the banging?' said Meg. A spray of tea shot out of Flash's mouth as he tried to stop himself choking.

'Banging!' he said, 'Banging! What sort of banging for Heaven's sake?'

'Well,' Meg said, as the old couple looked at one another for reassurance, 'after dark we put on the light, then the light goes out and the banging starts. It's just like someone with a wooden mallet knocking hell out of the wall, the ceiling, the floor and even this room's door.'

'But aren't you frightened?' said Flash.

'Nay, lad,' said Meg. It'll take more than a few Boggarts and Hobgoblins to scare us.'

'What's a Boggart?' asked Flash.

'My mam called 'em that. Ghosts I suppose,' replied Meg.

This was all getting out of hand Flash thought. Just a quick wiring job and now mixed up with the powers of darkness.

'Did you check outside and in the loft and other rooms for intruders?'

'Oh, aye, I did all that,' said Mr Barraclough, in a matter of fact voice.

Flash's mind by this time was working away like a demented computer. Eventually he came out of his reverie and said, 'I've got to get some advice on this.'

'Righto lad,' said Mr Barraclough, 'We understand. It's a right poser, so it is.'

Flash had managed to find a telephone kiosk a mile away from the house on the wind swept moor road. He managed to get through to his sister who was studying psychology at York University. She found a student with an interest in para-psychology. Piers, such was his name gave him some advice on the phenomenon.

'Do everything in a scientific way. Measure objects that might be thrown, weights, distances, angles. Check that strings aren't being pulled and keep careful notes of times of any happenings. Get a tape recorder or better still a camcorder.'

'Look, Piers,' interjected Flash. 'All I want to know is this blinking Boggart dangerous?'

'Our research on Poltergeist activity, which this seems to be, exclude serious assault.'

'What about minor assault?' replied Flash anxiously.

'Just scratches, bites and being pelted with odds and ends.'

'Well thanks Piers, you've cheered me up no end.'

'Happy to oblige and good hunting. Bye.'

Flash put a call through to his mum and to the agency to say he would be staying overnight as there was a lot of work to get through.

'If you hear anything in the night, ignore it, we do,' said Meg.

'Look Meg, I'm here to get to the bottom of this. Hiding in my bedroom won't solve anything.'

'Fair enough lad, but if you get scared come into our room, there's safety in numbers.'

Flash lay under the bed clothes fully dressed, a torch by his side. He held his hand up and looked at his fingers which were trembling slightly.

He must have dropped off because he was awakened by an almighty bang. The second bang, equally as loud made him jump out of his skin. God almighty, what had he got himself into. He switched on the torch and moved to the door. He was just about to open it, when he heard heavy footsteps on the stairs and changed his mind.

He looked round frantically for something to block the door with. The only thing was the bed, which he dragged over against the door. The heavy slow steps were coming down the landing now. They stopped outside his door. He could feel his heart thudding against his ribs. A mighty blow crashed against the door. The spittle in his throat looped the loop and he erupted into a paroxysm of coughing.

With eyes watering he called out in a high falsetto voice, 'Who's there?'

'Open the door to a spirit in torment,' came the answer.

Under his breath Flash's reply was, 'Not for an expenses paid month in Disney land,' would he open that door.

The blows stopped, all was quiet. He heard the footsteps moving further along the landing. Cautiously, he inched open the door and looked out. A glowing sphere about the size of a tennis ball hovered about four feet off the floor by the open door of the toilet. He eased open the door and went out onto the landing. The sphere had started to flash on and off once a second.

He crept up behind it. With a plop and a sizzle, it disappeared down the pan. With a smile he thought of the headlines in the tabloids, 'A Flash in the Pan'.

All was quiet for the remainder of the night. In the morning he said his good-byes and hoped the ghost had been drowned and would never return.

Falling in Love

by

Andrew Ure

'Don't let go! Please, don't let go!' yelled Colin in the most desperate voice you would never wish to hear.

'Whatever you do, just don't let go.' He was holding onto Laura with all his available might.

A real life or death situation had developed out of the Sunday afternoon walk - a walk which the couple so nearly skipped. If it were still raining, Colin would be in front of the TV watching the soccer, while Laura would be waiting on him and no doubt trying to lure him into the bedroom. But the downpour had stopped and the sky had cleared just as the last mouthfuls of their weekly roast dinners were being swallowed. Hence, after the customary 'Oh-that-was-lovely', coffee, and Laura's cigarette, the pair donned their jackets, jumped in the Cavalier, and headed for the cliffs.

Due to the rain the grass was very slippery. Far too slippery to be walking as close to the edge as they had been, but it's easy to say such things in retrospect.

'It's your fault we were walking so bloody close to the edge,' blasted Laura. 'I've a good mind to let go, and then you'd be sorry. Then you'd wish you hadn't acted so bloody macho wouldn't you,' she added rhetorically.

'Don't be a fool!... Anyway, what does it matter whose fault it was for Christ's sake - we're in this together aren't we? Just hold on to me tightly and don't let go.' But Colin could feel himself slipping.

Laura was a strong girl, but not strong enough. The two had been in their present positions for about five minutes now and Laura's energy was beginning to dissipate. Between them they had decided that just hanging on was the best option. Hanging on and waiting for some other Sunday strollers to amble along the path. Then they would shout for them to get help, and everything would be all right. At the moment, the grass on the cliff edge was so wet that any movement could result in the pair of them going over.

'Colin, do you love me?' asked Laura, penetrating the deadly silence of the last thirty seconds or so.

'Of course I do! You know that.'

'Then why have you lied to me? Why are you having an affair?'

'Pardon?' came a very shocked Colin. 'Why am I having an affair?' he echoed.

'That's right. Why are you...'

'Yes, yes. I heard you. Don't say it again.'

Colin really was very shocked. So much so that he had fumbled and almost lost his grip. How could she possibly know about that? He had covered his tracks perfectly, given absolutely no reason for suspicion, and been very happy for it. His silence gave him away.

'Don't look so mystified Colin.' She shifted her grip a little and glanced down. 'You didn't honestly expect to hide it from me did you? You must have realised that I'd find out sooner or later.' There was a short silence as they looked into each others eyes.

'Do you love her?' demanded Laura, very calmly.

'Look. This is neither this time nor the place to enter into such a conversation. There's bound to be a logical explanation for why you think so, but I'm not. I'm not having an affair. I'm not cheating on anyone. Can we just concentrate on getting ourselves out of the present mess first, and then we'll go into this ridiculous accusation.'

But Laura wasn't impressed by the denial.

'Colin, there's no point in denying it. I know, and that's all there is to it. I'd just like to know who it is that means so much to you and has ruined everything for me.'

'No-one's ruined anything Laura. No-one could ever come close to it. I love you more than life, Laura. Let's just get out of this mess, and then we can talk properly. Just hold on tight and don't do anything silly.'

Colin knew that Laura was planning something. He could see it in her eyes.

'Like what? Don't do anything silly like what? You mean don't let go don't you? Don't let go and spoil the little cheating game you've been playing on your wife. Don't let go and betray you like you've betrayed your wife.'

So what if he had been seeing another woman for the last six months or so. He hadn't gone out looking for an extra-marital relationship, it had come to him. Just because he saw a girl almost half his age once, or at the most twice a week, didn't mean he wasn't still in love with his wife. If anything, it had made his feeling for her stronger - partly through guilt and partly through rediscovering the pains of being intimate with someone with whom you share very little. He felt as though he hadn't so much betrayed her as protected her from his own insecurities.

The affair had made him happier, but only because that was all it was. He enjoyed the plotting and scheming that was involved in their meetings. He enjoyed the feeling of doing something that he knew was wrong. He enjoyed the double-life he was leading. It made him feel less like a Sales Representative and more like someone whom biographers would like to meet. Anyway, he was going to call it off soon because he'd had a gut feeling it could only lead to disaster.

'Whose idea was it to go for a walk today - mine or yours?' asked Laura. Colin noticed that her lips were beginning to lose colour and quiver.

'Yours I suppose. You knew I'd be quite happy watching the match.'

'Exactly! And do you know why? It was to do this.' And with that she let go. 'I love you,' she screamed while the distance between them grew rapidly.

Colin stared on in disbelief. Laura had just committed premeditated suicide under his very nose, and it all seemed to be his fault. The situation was so unreal and alien that it felt like a film. His head was swimming with freeze-frames and lines from the final scene. 'I love you more than life Laura,' he recalled.

All right, so that was an exaggeration. But Laura had been in the position to take her own life- and his as well if she so wished, so desperation had been called for. He would have said anything to keep her hanging on, and then tackle the problem of marriage when they were both back on terra firma. He would have done or said absolutely anything to avoid the problems and pain he now faced.

Colin looked inland and then out to sea. He felt as if he had nowhere to go, but that he had to get there quickly. He was desperate. In his confused and throbbing head he tried his best to evaluate the few options available to him.

There was only one thing to do, and it was going to be the hardest thing he had ever done in his life. He had to go to his wife. He was petrified of what may happen, what it may feel like, but he knew it had to be done. You have no idea of how something like this is going to unfold, but there is always one way to find out. You just have to do it. What would he say to her, assuming he was able to talk? How would he explain himself? Perhaps he wouldn't have to. After all, she loved him and he loved her. The fact that he had come to her would speak for itself.

Yes. He took a deep breath and looked up to the heavens. He had to do it. Alison was the only person he could go to, that was obvious. But how do you explain to your wife that the girl you've been having an affair with has just killed herself?

Flavour of the Month

by

Joan Peek

The light began to fade and a cool breeze blew on the incoming tide bringing salt to her lips and the strong smell of seaweed. She shivered slightly and like a tortoise, drew her legs beneath her, covering her lacquered toes with her skirt. In the cottage behind her a light snapped on, flinging golden nuggets across the sea. The chink of glasses and a whisper of garlic filled her with contentment. Soon he would come to her with wine and crusty rolls and cheese but for now she had this quiet time to herself, time to heal the wounds the last year had brought.

How could I have been so blind that I didn't see from the very beginning where I was heading?

His back was towards me as I entered the restaurant. I had no premonition that this meeting was to be any different from any of the others. The restaurant was crowded. Even if he hadn't been sitting at the table I had booked I'd have known he was my man. He was leaning forward studying the menu and his body radiated power and the same lean energy that all men at the top seem to have.

Amongst his dark curly hair I glimpsed his neck. Tanned and remarkably boyish for a man who had reached the pinnacle of his profession, a man who could call the very highest in the land his clients.

I liked what I saw and there were no warning bells telling me to take to the hills! So, with the pleasant anticipation of translating the succulent aromas that surrounded me into a satisfying meal, together with the added piquancy of the task ahead, I joined him at the table.

'Don't get up.' I put a restraining hand on his shoulder, 'I got fouled up in the traffic. Have you been here long?' He looked at me coolly, sizing me up. I knew he was wondering if I was up to the job. Given a pretty face and all the prejudices were there.

'I never tire of watching your river Thames.' His voice was attractive, New England I thought.

'Another drink?' He put his hand over his glass. 'We'll order now.' I said to the waiter, hovering attentively.

The food was delicious, as I knew it would be, the service excellent. I'd left nothing to chance. With the business side of the meeting concluded to our mutual satisfaction, we sat back with our coffee and brandy.

I cradled the glass in my warm hands. The current flowing between us was as potent as the brandy and made me loathe to talk on a personal level. Lights danced in his dark eyes and I knew he felt the same.

The raucous 'root toot' of a boat gave me the excuse to look away from him and for a time we watched the river craft in angry altercation below us. But it was no good.

As I put out my hand to pick up the bill, it touched his. I had never been so dangerously attracted to a client.

Was it that I couldn't see, later in my flat, or was I deliberately closing my eyes to the problems that lay ahead? Whatever the reason, with the clothes, torn from our bodies, festooning the room, I felt my naked body relax after the surging tumult of our passionate loving.

I'd gone against all my principles. I knew nothing about him, other than that he was a top advertising man, brilliant at his job. I didn't go in for 'one nighters' and I never slept with clients.

Yet here I was, after a business lunch, crucial to the company, acting like a schoolgirl with her first love.

Her body tensed, her fingers clasping and unclasping a stone from the beach.

Love. That was the word I was trying to avoid but it was there at the back of my mind all the time, clambering to be recognised.

I should have seen from the way he wore me, that long hot summer, like a prize medallion, that as head of Corporate Productions I was 'flavour of the month'. Just his 'successful lady', the envy of all his colleagues, that all that attracted him was my strength. He didn't want to know the real me, the gentle me, the weak me.

It was doomed from the start but I didn't see it. I was too dazzled by a brilliance and colour more exciting than I'd ever known. I felt brand new, my body more responsive, my mind teeming with creativity. I thought I had finally found the man I would spend the rest of my life with. That to him was a threat.

'Hey! Cool it! Whatever happened to freedom? I need my space, time to play the field before things get heavy.'

I held back the tears, trying not to let him see my life shattered at our feet. No comforting cloak of pride to cover my weakness, that weakness that had been my undoing. I was so sure he had wanted what I wanted that I read the signals wrong, refused to see the signs. I stood before him, raw agony in my face. He saw me for what I was.

'Look I'll leave a few things here. There's no hurry. Just as long as I can have a lady to stop over once in a while. We can be friends, can't we? After all, we are adults aren't we?'

The pebble stung the sea, scattering the golden coins.

If Adam hadn't breezed into my life again, from the other side of the world, just then, I don't think I could have coped. I'd probably have chucked it all in, all the hard graft for nothing, all the long hours, the struggle for power, wasted.

But he was there, as he has always been when I needed a friend, someone to pick up the pieces, a sympathetic ear at the end of the phone. Undemanding, knowing just how to handle me. It seemed natural to go down to the coast with him, for a break. Nothing heavy, just good friends.

'Won't be long. I'm doing the garlic bread!' Her body warmed to the soothing familiarity of his voice.

'So I gather!' Her teeth shone in the moonlight as she lay back, stretching her legs. 'No hurry. I'm perfectly happy!'

A Strange Tail

by

Rosemary Marshall

My husband is a mongoose. Now let me make it clear. He wasn't always a mongoose, though quite when or how he became one I can't recall.

Perhaps I should explain. I have nothing against mongooses. That's not the problem. The problem is that he is an uncommunicative mongoose. And morose. And bitter. He was never like that before. He was always the life and soul of the party. Always the joker. A match for anyone and anything. Not anymore. It's his illness that did it, of course. Changed him completely. Well, it's understandable I suppose. You can't be yourself if you're not feeling well, can you?

We were always different. Came from two quite different backgrounds. But it didn't seem to matter. Not before, well you know. We always got on like the proverbial house on fire. They say opposites attract. I was basically quiet and shy, but with a streak of a longing for adventure running through me. Maybe that's what drew me to him in the first place. He was *such* a charmer. Quite the ladies' man as they say. Not at all the sort I would usually fall for but, well, I was just drawn to him somehow.

All my friends advised against it of course. Well, it wasn't so much what they said, more what they didn't say. And the way they looked at me. You know what I mean? But I didn't care. I loved him and that was all that mattered.

We had a good life too at first. No children, but then we neither of us really wanted any. We were happy as we were. He was generous and loving and good around the home. We had a lot of fun together. He worked hard, and I worked hard too, keeping the place clean and tidy.

And then he became sick. Just a little at first so we hardly noticed it. But it became progressively worse. It got so bad I hardly recognised him any more, and his personality changed along with the physical changes. Then one morning I woke up and looked at him and realised what had happened - he had become a mongoose.

It was a shock, I can tell you. But it wasn't nearly such a shock as watching his personality alter and deteriorate before my eyes. That was what was so distressing. After all, what does the outside matter when it comes down to it? It's what's on the inside that counts. I don't know much about mongooses, but I don't think he's behaving like one. He's behaving like nothing on earth.

Between you and me, I'm not sure how much longer I can cope with it. I'm just an ordinary squirrel after all.

Midsummer Day

by

Jennifer Greenway

It was Saturday, and Midsummer day. Jason and Russell, known as 'Jay' and 'Russ' were two very bored thirteen year-old twin brothers.

'You two, come darn 'ere!' shouted Bert, their dad. He stood at the bottom of the stairs, his fat belly hanging over his trousers, with his braces stretching to their last bit of elastic. He pinged open a can of beer, 'I want you two art of 'ere, art from under yer muvver's feet, but I warn ya be back by four!' he threatened them with a clenched fist - 'or else!'

Jay and Russ darted under their father's threatening arm and out into the sun.

The two lads scuffed their feet along the dusty track that led to their favourite haunt, the woods. The birds suddenly flew out of the trees, the squirrels darted out of sight, their peace and tranquillity was now under threat. The terrible two were on the prowl, what mischief would they get up to? Jay threw stones up into the trees to scare the birds, while Russ charged on ahead and leapt over the fence into the fresh soft green un-ripened corn. He was soon joined by Jay and in no time they were on their hands and knees racing each other, leaving in their wake channels of vandalised corn. The point of this game was to discover at which part of the field they would eventually emerge.

Soon two heads thrust from out of the corn. They found themselves on the edge of a fairly steep slope. Down below was a stream twinkling and winding its way through the country side. The two boys, eager to out-do each other, raced in roly-poly fashion down to the edge of the stream.

The fresh cold water was inviting. Jay took off his hot sweaty trainers and swished his feet about in the cool water. He was soon joined by Russ.

Every now and then the flash of sapphire blue and brilliant emerald green of the dragonfly would perilously dart over their heads. Another game for the boys, as they would try and grab the dragonflies, just to see how many they could catch.

Russ was soon bored and sat up.

'Cor! Look over there,' he nudged his brother. On the other side of the stream on a round shiny wet stone was the biggest dragonfly they had ever seen. It was at least four inches long, with silvery wings and a long shiny slender body. The boys leapt across the stream, both grabbing and fighting over who was going to capture it. They both missed and the next thing they knew it was floundering in the water. Jay made a last-minute grab for it and scooped it up in his hand. He held it tight, but it wriggled so much he opened his hand to let it go, but it didn't fly away. They peered at it curiously.

'Throw it away,' Russ pushed his brother, 'it's 'orrible!' Then they heard a little voice, that sounded a bit like the Chinese chap in their local take-away.

'No, I need your help!'

Russ lifted his tee shirt over his head - he didn't want to hear or see any more.

The little creature continued; 'I need your help, it's Midsummer day and I must get to the Dell by four o'clock, if not I shall never be made a member of the fairy ring.'

'Fairy!' exclaimed Russ 'Bloody 'ell!'

The day's boredom was turning into an unbelievable adventure.

Jay whispered to his brother to 'belt up'. He was the serious one out of the two. Russ suggested they keep it and put it in a jam-jar and make some money.

'No you don't!' threatened Jay, 'I'm taking it to the Dell.' His eyes flashed a signal to his brother - 'come on, we'll take the short cut.' Jay tossed the little creature onto his head. They hurriedly put their wet feet into their trainers and clambered up the slope.

Russ followed on behind, pulling faces and calling her 'Tinker Bell.'

'My name is Cob Webb!' she haughtily announced.

'Oo ever 'eard of fairies anyway, I think yer an alien from space - a U.F.O.'

Cob Webb was kneeling on Jay's head.

'Just because you don't normally see us, doesn't mean to say we don't exist, we are an incalculable collection of invisible phenomena!'

'Yeh,' Russ was not impressed. 'An Unidentified Flying *Object*!'

He ran to catch up with Jay, whose intent was to find the Dell as quickly as possible.

The short cut meant crossing the motorway and wading across a large pond, not to mention climbing over a few forbidden fences.

They were soon chasing down the little foot path that lead them into the leafy cool valley, known as the Dell. The little creature excitedly flew off Jay's head and darted about.

'You must go, and I must rest, I have to restore my invisibility.'

'Aren't you gonna say ta?' I thought fairies granted wishes and waved magic wands,' Russ grabbed out at her, 'I wanna mountin bike!'

Jay grabbed Russ's sleeve and urged him on. They scrambled back up the footpath, trying not the trip over the large tree roots that twisted and protruded above the ground. Jay looked back and shouted to Cob Webb to put a spell on their Dad. They knew that he would shout at them and wallop them with his belt. Russ suggested that she turn him into a mouse, then they could buy a mouse trap!

It was well past four o'clock when the two boys sneaked in through the back door.

'All right you two come 'ere, where do ya think ya bin,' he rolled up his sleeves.

It was never any good telling the truth, nobody believed them any way. Jay shrugged his shoulders, what had he got to lose.

'Playing with the fairies,' he replied.

'What!' their father's face swelled with rage, his veins standing out like spaghetti junction.

'What's 'is name? I'll kill 'im, I've told you to keep away form those sorts!' The boys held their breath as they saw he was about to take his belt off, but for some unexplained reason he changed his mind, instead he picked up his tie, and looking at himself in the mirror he put it on.

The boys relaxed, he wasn't in such a bad mood after all. Suddenly he spun round almost toppling over! The boys ducked expecting the worst..

'Did you see that?' - He was pointing to the top of his head - 'She poked 'er tongue out at me!'

'Oo did?' the boys looked at him curiously.

He was in a state of shock, and could only manage a squeaky, 'A f.f.f.f.f.f.f.f.!'

'Fairy!' replied the boys, giggling. They looked at each other - 'an Incalculable Collection of Invisible Phenomena!'

A Little Knowledge

by

E L Amsdon

'Two second-class stamps, please.'

Miss Banister watched the post-mistress take her time to tear them off, then handed over the counter a pound coin. She waited while the change was as slowly counted out, then said, 'Thank you', and, tentatively, 'It's a lovely day, isn't it?'

The post-mistress grunted, 'Yes,' and turned to the next customer.

Miss Banister cycled home, fuming. Even after two months she still encountered antagonism from the village inhabitants, except from the Vicar's wife, who presumably ought not to harbour resentment.

Her anger lasted until she reached home, and settled down to her tea. She was just pouring out a second cup when there was a knocking on the back door. She answered it, to find herself facing a giant of a man----- quite a good-looking young giant too, with brown hair and blue eyes.

He knuckled his forehead.

'Afternoon to 'ee, Missus, but Oi 'eard you were a-wantin' some one ter do the garden.'

'Oh, yes,' said Miss Banister eagerly. 'Won't you come in, and we can discuss times and hours - and pay, of course.'

'Jest as you loike, Missus.' He stepped inside and into the sitting-room, then stopped and looked at the cup of tea.

Miss Banister, a little flustered, asked, 'Would you care for a cup?'

'Oi would thaat,' he said, and unasked, sat down by the table. 'Oi be Jem Forrester, Missus.'

Miss Banister poured him a cup, then sat herself in her usual place - an arm-chair.

'Now, when can you come?'

'On a Tuesday, loike today, Missus, 'bout this time. Oi be working all day at Yelmsgate Farm. An' Oi could do Thursday, too.'

'What about an hour and a half - or two hours a day, at least, for the summer?'

'Suits me foine, Missus.'

60

Miss Banister finished her tea and rose.

'Perhaps you'd like to see the garden.'

'Thaat be foine, Missus.' He finished his tea at a gulp and followed her into the garden. It was not large, but was packed full of plants. To Miss Banister it was untidy and messy.

'Now, Jem, I'd like all this cleared away.'

Jem frowned. 'But 'tis a cottage garden, Missus. Them be all garden plants. Them 'ull be in bloom soon.'

'I don't like heaps of plants. What *I* would like here are neat beds of roses, and perhaps some bulbs underneath for the spring.'

'Nothin' else, Missus?' He sounded amazed.

'No, nothing else. I should like you, on Thursday, to start digging out these plants, and then put in rose-bushes.'

He shook his head. 'Cawn't be done, Missus. Not this time o' year. Might kill 'em dead in 'ot sun.'

Well, the garden could be tidied now, and the roses left until September. Jem must have read her thoughts.

'Oi'll tell 'ee what, Missus. Oi'll tidy them plants for the summer, let 'em bloom, and get 'em out later.'

Miss Banister could only agree. So a rate for the job was settled amicably.

On the next Thursday he appeared just after half-past six. Miss Banister, drinking her second cup of tea, asked, 'Could you do with a cup before you start, Jem?'

As he drank, Miss Banister noticed that he was looking round, and seemed particularly interested in her book-case.

'Do you like books?' she asked.

'Oi do thaat,' he replied enthusiastically. 'Can Oi 'ave a look?'

'Help yourself.' She wondered which book he would pick out. To her amazement he took one on history.

'Oh, you like history, then,' she said. 'You can borrow it, if you like, read it, and return it on Tuesday.'

'Cawn't do thaat, Missus. No peace at 'ome. Me mam an' me Auntie Alice allus talkin',' and they allus shouts, bein' deaf.' He hesitated, then went on: 'Oi was a -wondering, Missus, if Oi could stay a mite a'ter workin' an' read 'ere. Oi wouldn't disturb you, Missus. I be loike a mousekin.'

Miss Banister felt embarrassed. To have a stranger - a man - sitting in her room for weeks and weeks was not how she had envisaged her evenings.

As she hesitated, he went to replace the book. She said quickly, 'Don't put it back. Please sit and read it here after you've finished gardening... I read too.'

There began a routine. Directly Jem had finished outside he washed his hands and settled down with his book. Every now and then Miss Banister stole glances at him. He seemed to be very absorbed, and read quite quickly, too. Just before he went home Miss Banister provided more tea and added sandwiches. Then he started sitting down in the arm-chair opposite hers, and ate his supper there, smiling at her when-ever she glanced at him.

Jean had been working in the garden for about two months when one evening, instead of saying, 'Good-night, Missus,' he remained sitting, and produced a pipe. He said, 'Opes you don' object, Missus.'

Miss Banister usually did not like the smell of tobacco. But the aroma from Jem's pipe was almost pleasing, so she did not demur. Though she had a sudden chilling thought that he was now making himself very much at home.

As if he again guessed what she was thinking, he said, 'Might be Maister an' Missus, eh?'

In a panic Miss Banister rose quickly.

'I... I'll have to say good-night to you now, Jem. I've decided to have an early night,' and waited for him to move.

He waved his pipe.

'You go up, Missus. Oi'll jest set 'ere an' finish. Oi'll lock back for 'ee when Oi go.'

Miss Banister could only make a dignified exit. Up in her bedroom she locked the door for the first time.

It could not go on. But how could she put a stop to Jem's routine? It was decided for her. One evening Jem knocked his pipe out in the ash-tray she had had to buy, and said, 'Oi wants ter 'ave a word with 'ee, Missus.'

Relieved, Miss Banister answered, 'And I have something to say to you, Jem.'

He beamed. 'Oi wondered when you'd arsk me, Missus. Folk be talkin' 'bout us. But we can make it alright by namin' day.'

'The day for what?' inquired Miss Banister, in a dazed voice.

'Day you an' me get spliced.'

'Married... you... and... me?' Her voice began to fade away.

'Oi seen you a-lookin' at me, Missus. Oi be a bit younger than you, but it don't signify. Oi'll be gentle with 'ee.'

Miss Banister's legs, which had been weakening gradually, suddenly got their strength back. She reared up, bosom heaving, finger pointing.

'Marry *You?* I've no intention of marrying you or anyone! I think you'd better go now.'

Jem looked bewildered.

'Then why did 'ee lead me on? Cups o' tea... sittin' 'ere with you... lettin' Oi read yer books... givin' Oi supper? Oi don' unnerstand.'

For answer Miss Banister marched to the front door and threw it wide open.

'You are to go now. *Now!* And don't come back... ever!'

Jem plodded to the door, and paused. But Miss Banister gave him a push, which made him stumble over the threshold and out into the twilight.

Left alone, she sank into a chair, shaking violently. After a minute she found a small bottle of brandy (for medicinal purposes only) and poured herself a stiff drink, then another. Later, in bed, she lay awake, seeing the scene downstairs again and again. Something would have to be done, and done quickly.

Some time later, after the moving van had departed, Miss Banister shut the front door for the last time, and prepared to follow the van in her car. As she turned the corner of the lane, she caught a quick glimpse of the Vicar's wife, Mrs Dunbury, with Jem's mother beside her, passing by.

'That was Miss Banister, wasn't it? I can't really make out why she's moving,' said Mrs Dunbury.

'But she be a bit queer-loike,' said Mrs Forrester.

'When she met Alice an' me she used ter shout at us... just as if us were deaf-loike.'

'Well, one thing, your Jem and young Sally Biggs will be able to get the cottage now. Don't let Jem hesitate *this* time.'

'Ee won't. An' there's another thing. Why did Miss Banister keep on at our Jem ter get 'im ter read dry old books? Anyone could 'ave telled 'er 'ee's always been dys... dysleptic, an' cawn't read at all.'

63

Her First Dance

by

M Collins

Jane knew, the moment she stepped into the village hall, that she had been right. It was a truly horrible dress.

Her first dance, without a watchful adult briefed to 'keep an eye on Jane'. So looked forward to, so many high hopes - and now - her dream had become a nightmare and left her wanting to run and hide. Oh, that hateful, hateful dress!

Her mother, undeterred by the look of stark horror in Jane's eyes, on first sight of the beastly thing, had dropped it into the cleaners, chattering excitedly to a very unresponsive Jane.

'I know it's not quite you now darling, but if I take the waist in, and maybe one frill to soften the neckline - oh, Jane, you'll look beautiful - the belle of the ball! And Mother had laughed happily - really laughed. Genuine laughter, Jane thought sadly did not figure too much in her mother's life. Oh, Dad and she adored each other, of course. But life had been so hard, bringing up two small girls since his accident. The strain of daily cleaning for others, and sewing far into the night showed in the violet shadows beneath her eyes, and the fine lines around a mouth made for laughter.

Jane later confided to her sister, Susan. 'You know how lovely it is to hear Mum laugh, Sue. I just had to pretend to be pleased, but I'll die, I'll simply die, if anyone sees me in that old fashioned thing!' Sue had been sympathetic but unhelpful. At ten years old, what she wore, providing it was suitable for scrambling up banks and swinging from trees, was a matter of complete indifference to her. Come to think of it, what anybody would want to go to a stupid old dance for in the first place, she really could not understand.

And so the dress was cleaned, and Jane despatched to bring it home for loving alteration.

'Oh, dear, love,' the fluffy little shop assistant had said, as Jane unwillingly produced her ticket, 'I'm afraid that's the one the dye ran in. We'll pay compensation, of course.' Jane's heart leapt. A leaden weight lifted, and she floated on a cloud of sheer relief.

The assistant was still talking. 'Oh, no it's all right. It was Bowen, not Rowen that was spoiled. Here's your dress. Pretty colour, isn't it.' An almost audible thump signalled Jane's return to earth. Dumbly she took the proffered parcel, and just managed a nod of thanks.

Defeated she trudged home. She stood mute through the fond pinning, snipping and stitching that followed, finally managing a brave, 'thanks, Mum, that's lovely.' Then with a quick smile -she fled ! In the safety of her bedroom, she cried - how she cried. Hot tears of rage and self pity.

'I can't go,' she sobbed into her pillow. 'I'll be ill - I'll run away! Oh, why can't parents understand!' Sleep proved impossible that night. She tossed and turned, pursued by witches, hobgoblins and demons, diving and wheeling around her head - and all in bright billowing chiffon! But morning had dawned relentlessly and had moved swiftly towards tonight.

Oh, if only Mother's friend had not given it to Mother for 'Jane's little do'. If only Mother had not been so glowingly happy to think of her dancing the night away in a dress such as she could never have afforded to buy her. And Dad, pride at rock bottom since his working life had come to a premature halt, smiling at her fondly, just before she left the house.

'You look sweetly pretty, my darling,' he had said.

'But Dad,' she had wanted to cry out, in fifteen year old frustration, 'Nobody in my crowd wants to look sweetly pretty. Sophisticated maybe - even daring - but sweetly pretty - yeuk!' But she couldn't wipe the happiness from their faces, and had swallowed the words unspoken, thanked Mother for the dress - and prayed for a miracle. It hadn't happened! And here she was feeling scared and silly on what should have been her big night.

She took off her coat, and surveyed herself balefully in the fly speckled mirror, which was all the hall boasted.

'You look,' she said accusingly to the reflection that faced her, 'exactly like a turquoise explosion!' In a frame of tumbled auburn hair, two large blue eyes stared back at her, with something approaching desperation in their depths. She couldn't, simply couldn't face everybody in floor length swirling chiffon. Why nobody wore long dresses anymore! What would her best friend, Anna say? She always had such fashionable clothes. And nasty Marjorie was sure to come. And not that he ever noticed her - but Steven might be there! At the thought of tall, dark, Steven Jones, Jane's heart missed a beat. The last of her hard won composure deserted her, and completely forgetting her coat, she made a panicky, despairing dash for the door.

'Ouch!' Her headlong flight was checked abruptly by sudden impact with a hard, lean body, and she looked up into the laughing brown eyes of Steven Jones. Of all people - Steven Jones! He raised an eyebrow comically.

'Hey, hang on Cinderella, it's not midnight yet, you know!'

'Yes, I mean No - I'm sorry - have I hurt you?' Jane stumbled desperately on, while trying to control her fluttering chiffon. Steven held out his hand and grinned ruefully.

'Prince Charming at your service and mortally wounded to boot, I claim this waltz as a penance.'

Without waiting for a reply, he seized her round the waist and swung her onto the dance floor.

'You know, Jane,' he whispered, lips against her cheek, 'You look different tonight - sort of romantic. I never noticed before how blue your eyes are.'

Marjorie danced by, casting Jane a look of utter loathing, and Jane's happiness was complete. She relaxed in Stevens arms with a sigh of pure delight, and gave herself up to the sheer joy of dancing. Surely lights had never twinkled so brightly or music sounded so sweet. She swung suspended in a kaleidoscope of colour and beauty, somewhere between the stars and the moon, as her feet followed, it seemed of their own accord, intricate steps she had never known she could do.

She glanced at Steven's handsome face, bent searchingly down to hers. Maybe her future lay with him, maybe not. But whatever happened now, time would never dim the sweet magic of this - her first dance.

A Winters Tale

by

Linda Melbourne

Shona was cold, wet and hungry. The snow had been falling steadily all afternoon and once night had drawn in, it was bitterly cold. Trudging through the snow, she had no idea of how late it was, or even where she was. It seemed as though she had been on this same road for days but in reality, it was no more than two. Hardly a car had passed her along the winding country lane all day and she had seen none since nightfall. Shona had never felt so alone.

Through the darkness, some way ahead, a light shone out its welcoming glow. Could Shona dare to stop? She was so cold and tired and the light looked so inviting that she decided to take a chance. It had been days since Shona had eaten, maybe beyond the light was the chance of food, Shona could almost smell it! Although the light had seemed welcoming, the old farmhouse looked so oppressive looming up out of the darkness that Shona almost turned back. A sharp stab of hunger gave her false courage and she continued to the door and knocked boldly. As she stood shivering on the step, her courage almost gave way as the large oak door creaked open. A shaft of light shone through as a voice from deep inside the house boomed out, 'Who's there Audrey? Another driver run off the road again? Be wanting a tow out with the tractor I suppose?

'No, no Fred, its some wee lass, chilled to the bone she is too.'

Audrey ushered Shona inside and following her, Shona found herself in a large warm kitchen. The man she presumed to be Fred was seated at a vast pine table in the centre of the room and as he turned to look at her, she was awed by how imposing he seemed but when her eyes met his, she could sense the kindness in his gaze.

'Well now, what's a wee lassie like you doing out on a night like this? You look awful hungry, will you be wanting a bite to eat?

Shona could only nod her head wearily as Audrey seated her in a cosy chair beside the Range where the heat radiated out, enveloping her. After two bowls of hot, steaming stew Shona felt her eyes grow heavy and begin to close. In the distance she could hear Fred and his wife talking in hushed tones. They were worried about someone so young being alone and were going to give her a bed for the night. In the morning they would contact the police to see if she was re-

67

ported missing, if there was no joy, they would send messages all over to try and contact her family.

Audrey roused Shona and took her into the sitting room where a cosy fire glowed in the hearth.

'I've made you a bed up in here dear, Fred has gone to fetch more wood for the fire, it should keep going 'till morning then.'

Shona lay down and let Audrey tuck the blanket in around her. It felt so good to be warm and safe once more that when Audrey turned in the doorway to ask 'by the way, what's your name love?' Shona was already fast asleep.

Shona dreamed of home, her family and the good times they had all shared together there. She dreamed of holidays and outings, especially to the circus - her second favourite place to home. Oh what a wonderful life she had! Into her dreams crept the fateful day she had tried so hard to forget. Her parents had always told her not to wander, to always let them know where she was going and to stay out of the fields at the bottom of the garden, especially since the Gipsies had moved in there. She had always heeded their words and stopped at the field gate but on this particular day, as she stood at the gate she saw a young rabbit playing in the field, making the most of the Autumn sunshine. The rabbit stopped to look at her and it seemed to be saying to Shona 'come play with me'. Without hesitating, Shona wriggled under the gate and raced off up the field after her new playmate when suddenly rough hands grasped her and lifted her off her feet. A gruff voice was whispering in her ear that she was not to make a noise or else and she was whisked away.

With a jolt, Shona awoke and sat bolt upright on the settee. Everything was strange and it took a moment for her to realise where she was, the fire had burned down and dawn had already broken. Shona recalled the hushed conversation of the night before, what if the police had already been called? In a sudden rush of panic, Shona leapt up, opened the window and raced off down the road. When she could run no more, she pushed through the hedgerow and into the thicket. Only when she felt safe from prying eyes did she scrape away the snow from beneath a tree and stop to rest, curling tightly into a ball to try and hold some warmth. What could Fred and Audrey be doing now? Would they have discovered her escape and telephoned the police? What if the Gipsies turned up and claimed her as their own? She must try to find her way home alone at all costs.

Her mind drifted to when the Gipsies had taken her, how could anyone be so cruel? She had been bound and thrown into a cupboard while the Gipsies had closed up camp and moved off. By the jolting and jerking, they had travelled many hours before they came to a halt and rough hands grabbed Shona from her prison. She was tied to a length of rope and allowed to exercise her aching bones, only a small bowl of broth was offered and she was too afraid to eat. The Gipsy children chased her and when the rope jerked her back, they all laughed and pelted her with rocks and stones. Only howling with pain brought relief as she was then trussed up and thrown back into the darkness of the cupboard. Life continued in much the same way for a week or more until one afternoon when the caravans had stopped in a village for water. Shona had been taken into the woods for exercise when an elderly couple had stumbled on them while out walking. In a panic, the two Gipsies walking her, ran back to the caravan and threw her into the cupboard without tying her up first. When the caravan set off again, Shona waited a while before opening the door and finding the caravan empty she leapt out onto the road, after rolling a couple of times, she bolted for the woods nearby. As the caravan was bringing up the rear, no one noticed her escape.

How many days ago that was, Shona could not remember, four or maybe five perhaps. Ever since, all alone, she had been trying to find her way home.

Wearily she got to her feet and, deciding to walk across the thicket and fields in case Fred and Audrey had raised the alarm, she set off. Around lunchtime Shona could hear muted traffic and crossing a clump of trees she could see cottages in the distance, could this be her village at last?

Shona hurried her pace and before too long, she was cutting across the gardens behind the cottages and came out onto a high street. Snow began falling heavily as Shona stood in front of a shop looking up and down the street. Glancing across the other side of the road, Shona thought she saw a familiar face amongst the bustle 'Mum' she yelled, and as her heart leapt with joy, she ran out into the road. At that exact moment a car approached, the driver slammed on his brakes as Shona ran out in front of him. He tried to control the car in the snow but with a thud, it skidded straight into Shona. The driver rushed around to the front of his car where a small crowd had gathered, he bent down and gingerly inspected Shona. Looking up at the crowd with tears in his eyes, he informed them all that she was dead. Never mind said one of the crowd - its only a dog.

In the shop window by Shona was a poster it read: *Lost Black Labrador. Stolen. Ex-Circus Animal. Can Do Tricks. Missed Desperately. Please Help.*

Underneath was a picture of Shona.

70

The Keeper

by

Daphne Hepton

'Have a good day.' Jack bent towards me. 'Happy?'
I nodded.
'God... the train must dash, see you tonight darling.'
I sighed contentedly and finished my coffee.

We had chanced on this delightful market town by pure accident and had immediately fallen for its quaint olde worlde charm. As soon as we found this little house we knew immediately it was meant for us. That's when everything seemed to miraculously fall into place. Jack got his promotion, we got married and moved out of the city and now here we were responsible mortgagors. If only gran could see me now.

This morning I decided to explore our new surroundings. I wandered around the dozen shops or so and then walked along to 'The Donkey's Ears', I smiled, it was a refreshing change from most run of the mill names.

The pub acted as a sort of full stop to the village, because there was nothing beyond but fields. Except for a narrow cobbled lane which I suddenly noticed running alongside it. Expectantly I turned into it although quite what I expected I couldn't say.

I was puzzled at the mist swirling about me as only seconds before the sun had been brilliant. Down at the extreme end a junk shop suddenly leaped out of the gloom. Delighted I hastened towards it.

Eagerly I pressed my face against the Dickensian panes, instantly my pulses raced.

There it stood, half hidden and very dusty but otherwise just as I remembered it, well not just as I remembered it, because this one couldn't possibly be *My* cabinet, the same cabinet which had stood ever since I could remember in a corner of my gran's sitting room.

How easily the memories came flooding back.

... I could see her now standing as she always did on the top front step waiting for me. I remembered vividly the endearing way her wrinkles deepened and

71

multiplied when she smiled and the way her short wispy hair was always put back, held with one hair pin.

Lovingly I would be drawn into her arms and held there so tightly that I could scarcely breathe, but she was so full of love and those first welcoming moments were so precious that I quickly learnt to hold my breath for as long as they lasted.

'Is it still here gran?' I would ask eagerly.

'Its always here luv 'til the day when you're ready, then and only then mind, it will be yours.'

I was about four or five when I first noticed the cabinet. I thought it a bit ugly. It was made of wood and painted a drab black, although it did have some carving towards the top. There was a plain glass door at the front with a small brass catch. When I was four it stood at least ten feet high but as I grew so the cabinet shrank, by the time I was twelve it had settled to a height of about three feet or so.

What delighted my childish heart was all the treasures that lay behind that glass door. Things which my grandfather had collected over many years.

Sometimes I was allowed to hold one object........

...'Have you been good?' And.. 'Then sit down luv...'

My gran repeated without fail.

Nodding fervently to the first part and immediately obeying the latter part the brass catch would be lifted. Carefully and with great deference the one article I treasured above all others would be taken out.

It was a beautiful slender letter opener brought all the way from France. Its silver blade gleamed below a white bone handle which felt wonderfully smooth and comfortable to touch. But the real magic lay in a pin prick size spy hole half way along the handle. It was necessary to shut one eye (which I managed to do by holding my hand over it) then holding the letter opener against my other eye I would peep through that tiny hole until I was able to see the Eifel Tower as real as if I was there. Magic indeed!

'That's in Paris luv, one day when you're grown you'll go there, just wait and see.'

I would look in awe. I could never imagine myself truly being there, why it must be at least a million miles away. In those days the only travel I had experienced was the journey, accompanied by my father, between our house in Kent and my grandmother's in Middlesex.

'Will you and the treasure cabinet be here for ever gran?' I would ask whenever childish doubts entered my head.

'None of us last for ever luv, not so's to be seen that is. But remember when God takes someone we love they stay always...in here.' And she would press her fist against her heart.

'Can I have that cabinet when you go gran?' I would ask with the innocence of childhood.

'Yes, but only when the time is right and not before young lady, your grandad, rest his soul made that 'imself. Yes, when the time is right.' A knowing wink always followed this mysterious statement. I didn't understand and she never elaborated.

But it wasn't to be, six months later she died.

After the funeral we trooped back to her house.

...'She didn't suffer, went quietly in her sleep.' Everyone murmured nodding their heads knowingly. The house seemed strangely unfamiliar without my grandmother's presence, I was far too old to cry of course, but when the tears welled up I ran into the garden so that no one could see.

I was horrified when I saw that most of my grandmother's lovely things had disappeared including the black cabinet.

'Aunt Agatha has had her vulturous claws on everything...' I heard one uncle remark.

'It's disgraceful and poor Matilda barely in her grave...'

So some awful aunt I didn't know, had taken my treasure cabinet away. Whatever would gran have said? Fresh tears threatened and I again retreated to the sanctuary of the garden.

'Now there'll never be a right time gran.' I had whispered. 'Our cabinet's gone for ever...'

But I soon found that gran had been right about one thing, that was that no one could take my precious memories of her away. I closeted them securely in a special corner of my heart. Thank-goodness the aunt Agatha's of this world couldn't steal those...

'Hello missy.' An old man stood close behind me. Quickly I shook myself back to the present.

'Oh, er, that black cabinet, could I have a closer look please?'

He smiled and shuffled off murmuring something about 'It's time...'

73

Pushing aside some books he dragged it out into the light. I gasped it was identical but it couldn't possibly be my gran's... could it..? Of course not... But what an extraordinary coincidence.

'I'll have it.' I blurted out unceremoniously, scribbling down our address. 'Could someone deliver it please?'

'Of course missy, we've been waiting...'

Puzzled I turned to ask what he meant... but he had gone. Bit strange I thought, but the trill of finding such a cabinet soon pushed the old man out of my thoughts.

Excitedly I hurried home only to find that the cabinet had already been delivered. Dumbfounded I started. It was in exactly the right corner. But how could they possibly have known that? And how had they got in? Perhaps I had left the back door unlatched? Easy to do in this tranquil little place which seemed so far removed from the necessary precautions of city life. Eagerly I polished the black wood and washed the glass door until both gleamed. Idly I wondered what had become of all the little treasures my gran had kept so lovingly.

I noticed an errant cobweb at the back and flicked the duster at it, there was a feint click. I watched in amazement when a small drawer slid open. My hands trembled when I saw what lay inside...

Almost reverently I lifted it out and automatically sat on the floor before running my fingers along its smooth edge.

'Oh gran,' I whispered.

I put the peep hole to my eye, the Eifel Tower stood majestic as ever. If only gran had known that I would spend my honeymoon there. There were so many questions, I must go back to the old man.

I searched everywhere until my head spun but the shop seemed to have completely disappeared. Exasperated I enquired at 'The Donkey's Ears'.

'Junk shop down Martyr's Lane?' The landlord stroked his chin.

'Old Jo Jenkins had a storage place. He kept things 'til folk needed them. They called him The Keeper. When he died they knocked it down. 'Aint been nothing there since.' He grinned.

'When did he die?' I asked.

'Ah, that's an easy one, cos it happened the day my sister got hitched and she's just celebrated her twenty fifth anniversary, it was the 10th of September...

My head reeled, my grandmother had died on the 10th of September exactly twenty five years ago...

The Cleaner

by

Hilary Scudder

Annoyed to find her hand shaking as she poured gin into a tumbler, Anthea began silently to justify herself. It was a welcome relief when the phone rang and she added a token amount of tonic before lifting the receiver.

'Hallo Penny, I'm glad you rang. I'm here all by myself, drinking gin and feeling guilty.'

'But you always drink gin darling.'

'No, it's not the gin, I've just - well, I've just done something dreadful.'

'Oh, Anthea - not the new Volvo?'

'No - I've fired Miss Hinks.' She gulped her grin.

'Oh, my dear, how brave - oh I do admire you. Don't you remember old Rose? How I kept trying to pluck up the courage to get rid of her? That woman terrorised me in my own home. She used to pursue me with that damned hoover and drop ash all over the house. I had to clean up after her. Five years that went on.' Penny's giggles of reminiscence tinkled down the line as Anthea sipped gin and sank onto the sofa.

'But I feel so guilty.'

'Guilty? Don't be silly, the woman didn't do her job. We've both said if cleaning only meant middles, we could do it ourselves. It's the edges and those awful corners that make it such a bore.'

Anthea began to feel better. 'It was when I mentioned her not cleaning in corners that she turned really odd.'

'She always was odd though.'

'Yes, I know, but she seemed almost manic, she started shouting and her eyes were glassy. I was quite frightened.'

'Poor you. I expect she'd come across something nasty. When I was doing my own cleaning, I found all sorts of - well, frankly things one would rather not find, lurking in corners. I just used to push the furniture back and leave it all there.' They giggled together.

'I'll have to find someone soon, I'd hate to think of things lurking in my corners. Anyway, Nigel does like the place to be clean and tidy.'

'Why don't you go out now and look in the shop window, that's where these people advertise, you know. I'm off to the squash club, I'll ask if any of the girls know a reliable woman. I must go darling, I'm terribly late. I'll ring you tomorrow. Chin up.'

Anthea drained her gin, got resolutely to her feet and went to find the Volvo keys.

Lorna Hinks was breathing heavily as she descended the concrete steps. She unlocked a door which opened directly into a room furnished lighthouse style, chairs grouped roundly together in the centre, sideboard and bookcase diagonally behind them, making the room appear circular. Her face was contorted as she dropped into an armchair.

'Why - why did she have to say that,' she raged to herself. 'Why mention cleaning the...' Tears ran down her face at the memory of the word.

'Lorna, Lorna, Granny's in the corner,' sang a voice in her head. 'Lorna Hinks, you are not paying attention. Go and stand in the corner,' said another voice, sharply. But instead of standing there quietly, she had screamed and screamed and they had sent her to a doctor.

The nurses at the hospital tried to be kind to the child. 'Come over here,' they said, 'to this nice bed by the window, in the corner,' and she had screamed. Standing there in the middle of the ward, making a spectacle of herself, screaming.

When eventually the nurse said to her mother, 'She can go home now, she's turned the corner, she'll be fine,' she did not scream. She was cured.

But when they got home, her mother said, 'Lorna, take Granny her tea, she's waiting.'

'Lorna, Lorna, Granny's in the corner,' they used to chant at school. And it was true. She never moved. Sitting in that dark corner, the smell of old lady and medicine hung like a shroud waiting to engulf you; the china pot on the floor, crumbs everywhere and always, in a sticky patch on the table, those teeth, leering.

Tears still streaming, Lorna struggled to her feet and turned to face the sideboard. 'You've done it now, you old bag,' she shouted at the space behind it. 'You've lost me my job. There'll be no money now, no food. Won't need your teeth, will you? You can starve and rot and leave me alone. I don't care.' She began to push the heavy sideboard towards the wall.

Anthea heard the key in the front door and hastily put her glass in the dishwasher. She picked up a tea-towel to wipe her hands and carried it with her out to the hall.

'Hallo darling,' Nigel kissed her and put his briefcase on the floor. 'What have you been doing today?'

'Oh, Nigel, I think I've done something very brave.'

'That's my girl - shall I pour us a little drink and you can tell me all about it.'

She followed him into the lounge and curled up on the sofa. 'I fired Miss Hinks,' she said, accepting a fresh glass of gin.

'Darling, that was brave. Such a strange woman, completely round the bend of course, better off without her. Always difficult though, firing someone. Clever girl.' He raised his glass and noticed the tea-towel on the arm of the sofa. 'Poor lamb - you've had to spend all day cleaning. I'll take you out to dinner, make it up to you. Go and change into something pretty.' He beamed at her. Anthea drained her gin and walked rather unsteadily towards the stairs.

'We'll advertise for a new cleaner,' Nigel was saying as he followed her. 'Can't have my wife turning into a drudge.'

She smiled and gripped the banister for support as he patted her plumply on the bottom.

The Stranger

by

Susan Vaughan

The black, velvety night descended over the countryside like a thick blanket, swirling about the car in a dark, impenetrable mist, its cold fingers seeping through the open air vents, touching her flesh with clammy fingers, stroking her hair with an amorous touch, compelling her to come and join it. Chirsty shivered once, briefly, and lent further forward in the seat, her tired eyes peering out into the gloomy night as the feeble yellow beam from the headlights picked out the deserted road ahead. Tall shadows loomed menacingly at the side of the road, throwing dark shapes across the meandering track. Bats fluttered overhead, their dark wings a soundless threat as they flew easily around the tops of the trees, screeching at each other with silent voices.

Chirsty shrank back into the soft leather seats and pulled the old cardigan closer to her slender shoulders, but the icy air penetrated the soft mohair, and she shivered again. Slowly, she put a hand out to the controls, and her numb fingers struggled with the stiff dials as she fought to close the open vents. Sighing with exasperation, she glanced at the road before bending down to examine them more closely. She wasn't used to driving her husbands car, and the complexities of the controls still mystified her.

The bump, when it came, arrived with a sickening thud, and a single high pitched yelp filled the still night air above the growl of the powerful engine.

'Dear God.' Whispered Chirsty, and her soft, beautiful face turned a deathly shade of white. She slammed her foot down on the brake, and the large car ground to a stop, its expensive tyres crunching on the loose grit at the side of the road. Slowly she put out a trembling hand and lifted the lock and a deep click resounded around the interior as the other doors sprung to attention. Taking a deep breath then letting the cold air sit in her lungs for a moment, Chirsty forced herself to relax. Slowly she opened the door, and climbed cautiously from the plush car, her elegant shoes slipping on the round shiney stones that covered the surface of the road. Holding her breath now, Chirsty made her way to the front of the car. She shut her eyes briefly, and put out a hand and gripped the cold metal to steady herself before she bent to take a look. For a moment her eyes refused to focus as the glare from the headlights blinded her vision, but then as she looked beyond the light and onto the road she felt the breath stick in her throat.

There was nothing there.

Chirsty blinked with surprise. She knew that she had hit something, something soft, something warm and solid. Something alive. But there was definitely nothing there. Slowly she ran a hand along the front bumper, and she felt a small, wet patch. She rubbed the tips of her fingers together and held them out in the light. Blood. But whatever she had hit had disappeared. Chirsty let the breath trickle from her mouth, and the warm moisture was lit up in white frosty clouds. It must have got up and run off. She felt the relief flood her tired body, and she took one more look before slowly making her way back to the drivers door. It was then that she saw the other car. It came up behind, fast and furious, its bright lights flashing with impatience. Chirsty blinked, stunned for a moment by its frantic pace. Suddenly she felt very vulnerable. She was a lone woman out in the middle of the night on a deserted country road. Quickly she scrabbled with the handle, flinging the door shut. The key turned easily in the ignition and the engine sprung to life, its powerful throbbing such a reassuring sound. She jammed her foot against the accelerator and the car bounced forward, its tyres skidding on the gravel.

Chirsty expected the car behind to slow down, but it did the opposite, it accelerated even faster, its bright lights shining in her mirror, blinding her. She felt the blood pump around her veins as the adrenalin began to flow, and her breath came in great, gasping gulps that racked her body. Suddenly she felt very light headed and the air coursing through the open vents was an unexpected pleasure as it brought her senses back down to earth. She felt very vulnerable and very alone. What would happen if her car were to stall and she couldn't start it, or it broke down. Chirsty let a shaky laugh escape. She was being stupid now, expecting the worst. Nothing would happen. She would drive home and he would never dare follow her there into the bright lights of her drive.

She glanced up again into the rear view mirror, and he was even closer this time, if it weren't for his headlights, she could probably have made out his face. Frantically he began flicking his lights on and off, then dipping them and raising them. Chirsty had heard of men who pretended that there was something wrong with cars just to get women to stop and then they would..., but her mind wouldn't comprehend the word. Rape had always been her greatest fear. She could never live if something like that happened to her. Just the thought of it sent cold shivers shooting down her spine. Her white fingers grasped the leather steering wheel, and her knuckles were stretched so taut that they became white and shinney.

The narrow lane turned a sharp corner and for a moment Chirsty thought she had lost control as the car skidded, its back swinging out so that it scraped the bushes at the side of the road. A small cry of fear escaped from her bloodless lips and her eyes opened wide with horror as she thought for a minute that she were about to crash, but then the tyres gripped the surface again, and Chirsty found that she had control. The monster behind swung easily around the corner as its driver shifted gear effortlessly. He put his foot down, and for a moment Chirsty thought that he was going to ram her from behind, but he stopped just short of her bumper. She breathed with relief and concentrated on the road ahead. Not far now. David would be home. There would definitely be someone at the farmhouse.

She knew this part of the road well and steered the car around the last bend. Frantically she put her hand on the hooter, keeping it there as the car swung into the large drive. She breathed a sigh of relief as immediately the front door swung open and David stood there, his thick frame the most reassuring sight in the world. She let a moan seep from the base of her throat and dragging the car to a stop she leapt out from the interior, almost falling as she staggered towards him. He was at her side immediately.

'Darling, whatever has happened.' His deep voice was warm and safe, and she flung herself into his arms.

'He was chasing me.' She managed to gasp as the other car pulled up into the drive, screeching to a stop. They both looked up as the driver flung open the door and raced over to where they were standing. Firmly David pushed Chirsty behind him. His red, rugged face angry now. He swung a powerful arm towards the strange man racing over towards them, and his fist met with a solid punch, the man staggered back before falling to the ground. He looked up in stunned surprise.

'No, you don't understand,' He grunted. 'A man got into the back of her car whilst she had stopped.' He gasped for breath. 'There was someone in the back of her car, I wanted to make sure that she was alright.' Chirsty put a hand to her mouth.

'Oh my God.' She whispered, her white face luminous in the still night air.

Slowly David and the stranger made their way to the car, its engine still purring gently. Carefully they opened the door and peered inside. It was empty, with the exception of a large pool of blood covering the back seat.

One Lip, Upper, Stiff

by

Tom Deery

'I say - excuse me - are you all right, old chap?'

'Oh yes, fine - fine.'

'Only I thought - seeing you lying on the pavement like that - you - might - be - a trifle indisposed.'

'No, I'm fine really. I'll be up in a minute - when I get the old breath back.'

'Oh well, that's fine then. Only when a chap sees a chap lying on the ground - in a pool of blood - a chap saying to himself, 'This chaps got a problem.''

'True, but thanks, no problem.'

'Well, - er - I'll be trotting along then. But you're sure you're not bleeding to death, or anything positively ghastly like that?'

'Not a bit of it - not a bit of it.'

'Oh well, that's all right then. As I just said, I'll be trotting along. Nice evening, don't you think - especially after this morning's rain? Incidentally, I hope you didn't mind me approaching you. I mean - I realise we haven't been introduced.'

'Don't worry. Formalities unimportant. But I think I'll have to ask you to help me up after all. Do you mind?'

'Not at all. Just lean on me.'

'Oooh...! Hurts a bit. Not too much though.'

'Perhaps I should call an ambulance-'

'No, no, no. I'll just toddle back into the club, and George will get me a stiff whisky.'

'I say, I'm not sure if I ought to mention this, but there appears to be the blade of a knife sticking in your back.'

'Ah, I thought so. Pull it out, there's a good fellow. Do you mind?'

'Of course not. Might hurt a bit, but here goes....'

'Oooh! Now that's damned civil of you. You deserve a drink. Come with me, and I'll get George to fix you one as well. 'Scuse me if I appear to be hanging on to your arm.'

'You're very welcome. Er - Now I hope you won't think I'm prying, but it's not every day that one meets a fellow lying on the pavement in a pool of blood with a knife in his back. So I must confess to being a little curious -'

'Oh, it was nothing of consequence. This bounder dashed out from the shadows and stood squarely in my path. Obviously from the lower orders. 'I want your money!' he demanded. 'Well, now, there's a coincidence,' I replied. 'So do I', and walked straight past him. it was then, I suppose, the cad came at me from the rear. And I stupidly fell forward, then rolled over on my back. He simply stood looking at me with the handle of the knife in his hand. Dumb isolence we called it in the Army. He made some attempt to get at the blade but suddenly cut and ran. Ah, George there you are! Pour me a double, will you? And let my friend have whatever he wants.'

'Oh sir - are you all right, sir?'

'What d'you mean, 'Am I all right?' Of course I'm all right. Hurry up with the whisky!'

'But sir, the blood!'

'Well you've seen a bit of blood before, haven't you? If you're worried about the carpet, surely our subscriptions are high enough to cover the cost of a bit of cleaning.'

'I think, I think -'

'Stop thinking, blast you, and pour!'

'Yes sir. Yes sir.'

The little man's hand shook while doing as he was bid. Then he disappeared to reappear very quickly with the secretary.

'Now Colonel English, whatever's happened to you?'

'Oh, I'm not going through it all again. My friend here knows the details.'

'We'll have to get you an ambulance.'

'No, no, no!'

'But yes, yes, yes! Simpkins - nine, nine, nine.'

'Yes sir, yes sir, yes sir.'

'Oh well, if you must. But I'm going nowhere until I've finished this whisky. Cleaning me up might give 'em something to do. But I've got to be at Lords tomorrow by noon. Well now, my friend, I don't think I caught your name ....'

'Pomeroy, sir - Percival Pomeroy.'

'Pomeroy, indeed! We had a Pomeroy in the Guards. Damned good officer. But he was sent to some God-forsaken out-post of empire where the rations couldn't get through, and he died of alcohol deficiency, poor devil. Sorry for bleeding on you, by the way. Get your suit cleaned tomorrow, and send the bill here to be charged to my account. George, I'll have another of the same. George! George, where are you? Great Scott, I think he's passed out! George, stop dying or whatever it is you're doing down there on the floor, and attend to your duties. My glass is empty! Where's the secretary fellow, Blatherington or Bletherington or Blitherington - I can never think of his blithering name. Ah, here come the ambulance wallahs. Over here, chaps. Him behind the bar - heart, I think. Handle him with care. We want him back. He mixes a good bloody mary.'

George sat up and half opened his eyes. He peered across at the colonel.

'Blood! I can't stand the sight of blood,' he said and fainted again.

The leading ambulance man looked put out.

'Now come on. Don't muck us about.'

He looked straight at the colonel.

'Gawd mate. You're in a right mess, ain't yer'

'I cut myself shaving.'

The secretary burst in.

'Ah, you've arrived at last. I was just 'phoning again to say how urgent it was.'

'I'm going nowhere, Bletherington, until I have another drink.'

Mr Blitherington went behind the bar, stepped over the inert George and re-moved a bottle from the shelves.

'Here, you may take this, if you promise to go with these gentlemen at once.'

'Blatherington, Bletherington or Blitherington you're a gentleman after all. I may not always have thought so. I may not always have said so. But I'm think-ing so and saying so right now.'

'Can I just take your jacket off, squire?'

'No you may not!'

'We just want to do something about that wound.'

'Oh, well hurry up about it.'

The colonel's wound was dressed.

'Meet me in here tomorrow evening, Pomeroy. We'll have a longer chat. I've a suspicion that we're related. You've got my blood on you - you could also have it in you - who knows?'

'Try standing up a minute guv. We want to see if you can walk.'

The colonel did so but immediately collapsed. The medic intercepted his fall, but the old soldier was ungrateful.

'All right, all right! I may have had a few, but I'm not incapable. By the way, young man, did you shave this morning? It certainly doesn't look like it. Do you know - the Guards shaved every morning and lined up for inspection even during the fiercest bombardments of the war? We need another war to smarten things up again. Right, now you'd better let me have your arm. And your duty is to make sure I don't drop this bottle. Right, off we go. Heads up, shoulders back and stomachs in. Don't forget, Pomeroy - tomorrow evening here at twenty hundred hours, sharp!'

A Message to Mother

by

T Hodson

'Hello! Hello, Mum! Are you there? ... Allo!

'Oh why doesn't she answer?

'Mum! Hello!

'Mum!... Dad! ... Whoever! ... Will someone, please say something!

'I don't know why she does this!

'Ah! There you are, Mum! What on earth have you been doing?

'Yeah! Yeah! Okay! ... Well, you could at least have said '*Hang on a minute!*' It's so annoying - not to say worrying - waiting while you find yourself a chair ... All the time not knowing what's going on! Anyway, how are you?

'Oh! How long have you been like that, then?

'Well, you will just have to go and see the doctor.

'What do you mean, you don't trust the doctor?

'That's ridiculous!

'Yeah! ... Yeah! ... Well, you'd better change to another then.

'Oh, Mum! it doesn't matter that the new one won't know you! He'll have your records and everything.

'But ...

'Yes, you do need to have it seen to ...

'Of course ... All right!

'Anyway, how's Dad?

'Hello! Hello, Mum! Now where's she gone? Mum, are you there? Oooo! Oooo!

'Oh! Hello, Dad! ... Er ... where's Mum gone?

'No, no! It doesn't matter, but I didn't actually say I wanted to speak to you! I only asked how you were.

'You are! ... That's fine! ... Good!

'No, I don't suppose you have. It's all the rain we've been having. Still, it will do the crops good!

'Eh? What?

'Who mentioned a girl?

'No. No, I didn't say anything about a girl. You must have misunderstood me!

'Look, Dad, whose this girl I'm supposed to have mentioned?

'Loraine! What Loraine? ... Oh, Christ! You silly old fool! What I meant was ...

'All right - I'm not shouting! What I said was the rain ...

'You couldn't go to your allotment because of all '*the rain*' we've been having!

'Are you wearing your deaf-aid, Dad?

'I said: are you wearing your deaf-aid?

'I'm not shouting, Dad! I've got to speak up for you to hear me!

'Yes ... Yes! I know you're not deaf!

'Is Mum there? Will you put her back on the line, please!

'Yes, I know she is fine! I've just been talking to her!

'Tell her I want to speak to her.

'Dad, tell Mum ... Mum, Dad! ... I would like to have a word with her. You understand?

'I want to speak to Mum, Dad!

'God! I think it's sunk in!

'Hello! Hello, Mum!

'Yes, it's me!

'Eh! What do you mean?

'No, I haven't rung you again - this is the same call!

'No! Christ! *No* - it's not!

'Sorry, Mum - I didn't mean to swear!

'Mum, don't you remember? I spoke to you a few minutes ago and I asked you how Dad was, and you then put him on the phone - remember now?

'Yes, yes! It's the same call! Now look Mum, I want to pop over and see you.

'Yes of course, and Dad! Will that be all right?

'What for? What for! Well, I want to see you - that's what for!

'No, *No!* I'm not in any trouble! What a thing to suggest? I just need to see you - that's all! ... Nothing to worry about!

'When! When will it suit you?

'I know you don't go out! ... But you do go shopping!

'No, I wasn't actually thinking of coming over during the day. One evening. How about Tuesday?

'Surely, you don't watch Eastenders - do you?

'All right! What about Wednesday?

'Look, Mum, it's your son wanting to see you! You'll just have to miss Coronation!

'Oh, God! Look, if necessary, I'll only talk to you during the adverts!

'Please Mum, I'm not losing my temper or shouting! I just thought you'd be happy for me to visit!

'Eh? Well, actually I've something to tell you ... It's nothing really.

No, I rather not say anything now. I"ll tell you all about it when I come on Wednesday.

'No, no! I promise you, it's nothing serious....... Important, yes..... but nothing for you to worry about.

'Look, Mum, calm down! Don't talk silly! Just take it easy and don't get yourself into a state!

'No I won't give you a clue! I'm not saying another word about it, 'til I come over.

'Oh, God! Why did I open my big mouth!

'Sorry, I can't, Mum! Not over the phone - it's too delicate. You'll know all about it Wednesday.

Don't be ridiculous, of course you'll sleep!

'I don't know why you're getting all worked up. It's something and nothing!

'Look, I prefer not to discuss it over the phone - and that's final!

'Mum! Please Mum, calm yourself down!

'Well, all right, if you have to know! But don't forget, I'm only telling you because you insisted! It's, I'm we're emigrating to Canada! Now you know!

'No! No Mum! Birds migrate!

'Oh, God! Mum I'm not doing it to break your heart! You musn't say silly things like that!

'When? Two weeks Friday.

'Yes, I know that's not much time. That's the way it goes: you have to be accepted, then you go when they say.

'Don't you think, if I could have made a decent life for us here, I would have!

'You've forgotten, I've had no offers since I was made redundant. Anyway, this country is dead - well, it is for us!

'Please don't cry Mum! ... I'll miss you too!

'Yes, yes! Both of us and the children. We"ll miss you and Dad - we will, Mum!

'I don't think it's selfish to want the best for your family.

'All right! Of course, I know, you're family too.

'Try to look at it this way, Mum: with the cheap flights, it's not so far away.

'Yes, yes! You'll be surprised - you will do it!

'Look, when we've settled down, and I've got myself established in a good job, I'll send you the fare and you and Dad can come for a nice long holiday. Now won't that be something to look forward to?

'What's that?

'Of course, I won't be able to force you! You're just being stupid, now.

'I'm sorry, Mum. I apologise. Stupid wasn't the right word. It's just that in time you'll think different - you'll see!

'Now that sort of talk makes me angry! It's not all her doing! And while we're about it: isn't it time you called your daughter-in-law by her name. She is my wife, after all; the mother of your grandchildren!

'Now stop all this silliness, or I'll put the phone down!

'Be honest, Mum, you've never really liked her! ... And she thinks such a lot of you and Dad!

'Now that's unfair! I know you and Dad are getting on and won't be around much longer.

'Sorry I said that - but it was what you meant!

'Yes, I know! I do know! I really do!

'You have! I know you have!

'Oh, God! I wish I hadn't said anything!

'Look Mum!

'Yes, the best - haven't I always said!

'But......

'But, look Mum!

'Mum look! Hold on a minute, I've been a good son too! I didn't want to bring this up - especially now, on the phone - but I've been good to you. Always running you and Dad about: to the shops, holidays, hospital appointments, family visits and days out. Then there's keeping check on your financial matters. I've done my bit and you can't deny that! I didn't want to mention this, but isn't it time Ron and Elsie done their share? Over the years they've always been too busy. Well, now's the time for them to shoulder some of the responsibility. I hate to say this, but I've always felt you favoured them more than me: making excuses for them when they forgot your birthday, or were too involved with more important matters to run you to the hospital. Well, without me around they will have to do their share.

'What's that, Mum?

'What do you mean: *'Who's Ron and Elsie?'*

'Oh, God! Her brain's going!

'Listen, Mum! Ron's your eldest and Elsie's your youngest: my brother and sister! Surely you know that?

'Mum, if you're trying to blackmail me by pretending you're ill - it won't work! Nothing will stop me from going. My mind's made up, whatever happens, we're going!

'Oh, Mum, you really are the limit! Next you'll be telling me you aren't my Mum: Florrie Simcock!

'What's that?

'You're not! ... You're having me on! I must say, you've always been one for a good laugh!

'Oh, Christ! She's gone round the bend!... Say that again!

'Have I got it right: you say you are Gladys Brown?

Ah-ha! If that's so, what's your telephone number?

'It Is? ... Oh! ... I'm sorry Mrs Brown, it seems I have the wrong number!

'Eh?..... No sorry, I won't now be popping in on Wednesday!'

Inch Pinching

by

Effie Dimmock

It was the sideways look that did it. From the front Pauline looked 'comfortable', but as she turned, the curve of her tum filled the mirror.

'That can't be all me,' she exclaimed in horror to herself. But try as she did to conceal the fact, there were the tell tale signs of fat.

'Pinch an inch' the TV advert said. It was more like a handful.

'Why haven't I noticed this before?' she wailed to her friends.

'Because you've been too busy,' was the general reply.

It was true she'd looked after her neighbour's children while Nora was in hospital, done shopping for the old lady down the road, acted as secretary for the Resident's Association and found time for a few other odd things.

'Perhaps I've not been eating properly. I'll go on a diet.'

But which one? She found a bewildering array from which to choose. The Conley diet, the Hayes diet, eat no fat diet, take no sugar diet and a whole lot more.

Friends weren't much help either.

'Don't eat between meals, no snacks, no fat, no this, no that.'

'I know. I'll go and see the doctor,' but he wasn't much help either.

'You're a perfectly healthy woman. All you need is a little exercise.'

Pauline thought she had plenty of that in her busy life. Normally a cheerful person, his diagnosis brought her no comfort. On the way home her steps grew slower and slower.

'Was it her fat weighing her down?' she wondered. Perhaps exercise was the answer. She was always busy but perhaps she needed to go to a class. With a lighter gait she hurried home, determined to put his words into practice. Perhaps the local library had some information.

The girl was helpful and supplied a brochure. At home Pauline studied it with care.

Aerobics? Not for her. These lissom lasses cavorting to pop music made her wince just looking at their contortions.

Keep Fit sounded better. Over 50's Group, Exercises for the Older Woman.

90

Any of them were suitable, but none were near home. She didn't fancy a journey after unaccustomed gymnastics.

Scanning the list she saw there was a Medau Class at a small hall near home. The name sounded familiar. Wasn't that where Joan went? If Pauline could end up with a figure like her friend's she'd be well pleased.

A quick telephone call confirmed that was the one she attended. Joan said the exercises were gentle and she'd be happy to give Pauline a lift home.

'Wear something light,' she advised 'you'll soon get warm.'

After trying on almost her entire wardrobe Pauline settled for a tee shirt and trousers. When she arrived several ladies were already there removing their outer garments. Black leotards were worn by the majority, with one or two of the slimmer ones venturing into colour. She noticed with some satisfaction that there were others with layers of fat. She looked round for Joan but there was no sign of her.

'You're her friend?' asked the teacher, a slight figure who was peeling off her clothes to show a dazzling emerald leotard. She reminded Pauline of a caterpillar.

'Joan can't make it tonight,' she said. 'Welcome to the class. We always like newcomers. I hope you'll enjoy it.'

This was an encouraging start. The others gave her friendly smiles as she lined up with them.

'We'll walk round the room - barefoot if possible -' There was a short pause as Pauline removed her shoes. She wished Joan had warned her of this. Her nylons were a little slippery on the wooden floor, but she was sure that wouldn't be a problem.'With our heads held high, shoulders down and tummies in. Now in a line, move to the right, crossing one foot over the other as you progress.'

She demonstrated how it should be done. It looked very easy. The class sailed across the room with Pauline in the middle. Apart from the odd stumble, she managed quite well.

'This time, extend your arms to touch your neighbour's shoulder and move to the left.'

This was more difficult. They looked more like prancing cart-horses. Pauline's nyloned feet skidded and she fell into the lady on her left. She in turn bumped along the line and the lot went down like dominoes.

Sylvia, the teacher, didn't even blink, but said, 'Make up in pairs.' Taking the new girl by both hands, she told her to hold on firmly. Bending her knees, with Pauline holding her she went down on her haunches.

'Now you try,' she ordered. To Pauline's amazement, she was able to move without knees cracking. Sylvia passed her on to another partner. Together they seesawed up and down to the music. A few more simple exercises and she became more confident. She began to recall the ones she'd done as a child. No problem.

'Bring on the balloons,' said Sylvia.

'Now I want you to roll them round your body, first from right to left and then reversing from left to right.'

Apart from chasing her balloon a couple of times Pauline managed quite well.

'Now walk in a circle throwing up the balloons and catching them as you go.'

Pauline was sure her balloon had a life of its own. It appeared to drift along the ceiling and took ages to come down. Busy watching its progress, she stopped walking. The woman behind cannoned into her and they both went down in a heap. With a sad sigh the balloon collapsed and burst on her tum.

'Get her another one. We'll try again. At the end of the line where I can see you,' she ordered.

Only Sylvia was aware that her new pupil was having to dash backward and forwards to keep up with the rest.

'All of you to the far end of the hall. Throw your balloons forward, run and catch them till you reach me.'

By this time Pauline was becoming self conscious at her lack of skill.

'I'll take this one slowly,' she thought, but the new balloon dropped smartly and she had to chase off to the side to rescue it.

Sylvia watched in fascinated horror as another pupil got into difficulties and they rushed towards each other not looking where either was going. The collision landed them both on their backs with feet int the air.

Beyond a tightening of her lips, the teacher showed no emotion but ordered her class to bring on the mats.

'We'll do some floor exercises. You too,' she added turning to Pauline.

'I thought I'd sit this one out.'

'See what you can do,' was the brusque answer.

Stretched out on the foam carpets, the class cycled on their backs with legs in the air, curled into tight balls and did other strange convolutions. Pauline, aware that she was getting tired and puffed, pushed out a feeble leg now and then to look willing. For the rest of the time she was content to watch - and rest.

'Right. One more walk round the room and we're finished.'

'Finished.' What a sweet sound the word had. Pauline followed the others but hers was more of a stagger than a walk.

'You certainly tried hard,' one of the class said.' Shall we see you next week?'

'Maybe.' She was non-committal. The way she felt it was unlikely she'd survive the night.

'A good hot bath after the first lesson stops you feeling stiff.'

'I might try that. Bye.'

She made her weary way to the exit. No one offered her a lift.

'If only Joan had been there,' she sighed.

It was a struggle to get home, pushing one leg after the other. The stairs of her flat became alpine mountains to surmount, the hard settee a seductive goal. It creaked in sympathy with her as she sprawled across its battered leather.

Her usual common sense told her she shouldn't linger there too long. She wished she hadn't been so enthusiastic.

Hadn't Joan told her about taking it easy the first lesson? If only she'd remembered.

With a feeling of great weariness, she ran a hot bath and fell into it. Each pore, muscle, and bone eased in grateful thanks at the touch of the soothing water.

After a deep sleep, she woke to find she was still alive. Apart from a little tiredness, there was no ill effects.

'Keep it up,' advised her friends, when she recounted her experience. 'It'll get easier as you go along.'

But Pauline had made her mind.

'I'm going to exercise my brain, not my body. You'll have to put up with me as I am.'

No one seemed to mind, and Pauline enrolled for another class. The subject? 'How to have a healthy mind in a healthy body'.

The Traveller

by

Sobia Quazi

He got on at Barons Court, and immediately everybody looked. The woman with the crossword removed her glasses and peered closely. The man with the black coat, briefcase and newspaper uncrossed his legs, shuffled uneasily. The girl reading Miltons 'Paradise Lost', wholly abstracted until now, sensed something anachronistic and pushing back her hair, raised an eyebrow. Even the fat woman with four shopping bags stopped her aeroplane-landing snoring, and looked up in surprise. Yes, it was immediately obvious that he was from somewhere else.

You see, nobody usually got on at this stage. And then, suddenly out of the calm sunny day there was this strange visitor with a white bowler hat and cream-coloured trousers with no crease down the centre.

No accessories, no cheap effects. He was as he stood, frank; with hollowed eyes like the bottom of the ocean, a deeply bronzed face as if sculpted from rock. He deliberately stood, letting the silence build. Outside calm, the midday sun. Inside, silence... and him. There was a choked gurgle from a wide-eyed infant as a hand was hastily placed over its mouth.

Then the doors skimmed shut, there was a sharp wheeze and the tube began to edge forward. Meanwhile, they stared. The girl, the women, the executive - and many more besides. Outside, the sky slightly grey, darker. Inside, the tube rattling forwards, forwards, faster and faster. While he stood in the centre holding no rail, still as a rock.

And then it happened. He lifted his hat, shook his hair the colour of sand, and opened his mouth to laugh. He laughed revealing ordinary white teeth and a black hollow; laughed on, revealing stalagmites and a black cavern; laughed and laughed until there were ice-bergs in a pitch-black gulf. And the tube, rattling, hurtling down into a black chasm while he stood still, laughing.

By now it was obvious what he wanted.

'This metallic worm goes straight to Earth's gut. Any passengers?'

Outside there was blackness filled with the explosions of clashing meteors.

94

Inside there was silence. And in that silence it became apparent that he was from the mystical otherness, come to reclaim. He looked around, his gaze selecting people out.

'I've got three little kids, a husband...... and a lover.'

This was the large woman with several heavy bags. She spoke in a pleading tone. But he merely smiled.

'And me.' It was the executive. 'I'm destined for a promotion next Monday - a new position of power in my office. Two months more and I'll be Executive Manager.'

(but again, the smile)

'All that is material, it is as nothing compared to what I can give you. All of you.'

'At least give me a chance to ring my boy friend and tell him.' As she clutched Miltons 'Paradise Lost', even closer.

But with his hat, he made a swipe of his arm, pouring forth wooded glades, sunsets of orange buff and xanthous yellow over crumpled golden seas of rustling leaves, honey-scented orchards with sparkling streams; a night, soft blue scattered with myriads of silver specks. And especially for the old man in the corner who had been standing - an expanse of whiteness above a pine-forest; worlds zenith.

At Earls Court there was a rush of people, a chaotic sea of struggling potential passengers, as well as the odd clusters of tourists with their man-size backpacks striving to stay in one group. There was a gradual shuffling forward as the tube drew to a halt; and then, a forward surge, apparently at random. At least that is, until they spotted the one empty carriage, near the end.

The Surprise

by

Barbara Collett Aldridge

She bathed quickly and then lay back in the warm scented water and looked at her body critically. She had put on a stone in weight since her hysterectomy and it was clearly visible around her middle. She must go on a diet she thought.

After her operation John had arranged for her to go to New York to visit her sister 'for a long holiday to convalesce' he had said. It was there that she had left Ben, who was lost to her for ever.

The telephone rang, hastily she climbed out of the bath, wrapped herself in a towel and picked up the telephone from her bedside table. John had answered already, she was about to replace the receiver when she heard a woman's voice 'John about the eighteenth .....' he interrupted 'We'll discuss it tomorrow, I don't want Nancy to know about it yet, she's upstairs at the moment.' Carefully she replaced the receiver.

She had recognised the woman's voice as John's secretary. The eighteenth was their wedding anniversary, she thought he had forgotten, but it seemed he was planning to surprise her.

She felt reassured, since her return from the States nothing had seemed the same. Her daughters, Nicola and Julia had grown considerably, which was hardly surprising since they were both in their teens. John too was different, he was remote from her, there was a distance between them which she could not cross. In the afternoon while he watched television, she allowed herself to remember Ben.

She had met him at a dinner party her sister had given. Associate Professor of Art History at Lattimer College, a widower about fifty with thick dark hair lightly streaked with grey and deep brown eyes that seemed to look into her soul.

The following day she had visited the Metropolitan Museum, to view the exhibition of Cubist Art. After a general look around she was drawn back to 'Jeune Fille a La Mandoline'. Although the subject was fragmented into various shapes and facets it was clearly discernible. The separate surfaces seemed to move from their natural positions and slide behind, towards and into each other, so that at times the subject became part of its surroundings and at others to stand out from it, the effect was both stereoscopic and one of movement, it was as though the artist had viewed his subject from many aspects and then blended them into one on the canvas. She had liked the very nearly mono-chromatic colour scheme of grey, black, brown and ochre, lightly tinged with green and white, which seemed to add to the un-natural quality of the painting.

Then she had heard his voice at her shoulder,

'Hi there, what do you think of it?'

'It's an interesting painting that needs to be thought about as well as looked at,' she had answered.

'Sure and it's beautiful, almost lyrical,' he had said 'a valuable document of its period, 1910 in fact,' he continued. He had gone on to give her more information about Picasso's 'aesthetic intentions and his 'technical procedure'. Later they lunched together and discovered other interests in common.

The next few months had been wonderful and they had grown very close. One evening while returning from the theatre he had asked, 'why do you never speak of your husband?'

She had found it difficult to explain. She couldn't say that she and John had grown apart, that there was no longer any magic in their relationship. And now she had met Ben, who stirred a new feeling within her, she dared not call it love. He took notice of her, made her feel special, something John had not done for a long time. She said, 'I suppose it's because I feel such guilt when I think of him, because I enjoy being with you.'

The he had told her that he loved her and that although he had known from the beginning that she was married and had two daughters, it had made no difference. He had no doubts, for him there was only this moment, for her there was tomorrow Nicola, Julia and John. She struggled with her confused feelings and gently told him that her relationship with him would have to end before it became tarnished. She watched him leave and knew she would always hold him in her memory.

The following morning she arranged her flight home. The emotional upheaval she had felt was profound, it was as though a part of herself had died when they had parted. She had found it difficult to hide her distress from her sister.

The next two weeks she threw herself into a diet. She found a print of Manessier's 'Mistral' which she had framed as an anniversary gift for John. But nothing eased the pain of thinking of Ben.

The morning of the eighteenth was a Saturday. She awoke early and looked from the window, the garden was silent with the freshness of early morning, the December sun shone icy and clear and the black tracery of the winter trees stretched naked across the cold sky, the frost on their branches glittered like thousands of tiny jewels. How beautiful it all was, she thought.

She hurried downstairs and put the kettle on. While she waited for it to boil she prepared scraps of food for the birds, she put out fresh water and returned to the house to watch as they fought for breakfast.

An iridescent pigeon strutted towards the bird table while the smaller birds retired to the cover of a nearby shrub, hoping no doubt that the larger more powerful bird might leave a few crumbs. However the pigeon was unlucky for he was seen off by a squirrel, who sat and ate what he could and then made off with the largest of the remaining pieces. Just like people she thought sadly.

The postman's knock brought her back to reality, there were anniversary cards from the girls, from her mother and from John's Mother. John's card was a beautiful watercolour of a summer garden. He thanked her for twenty years of happiness and wrote that he would love her always.

When he came downstairs he took her in his arms,

'You look lovely today,' he said 'I've booked a table at the Green Room for the four of us.' Nicola and Julia were thrilled, they loved going out to dinner, the rest of the day was filled with excitement.

She gave John his present, 'Darling it's wonderful' he said.

She asked him where he would like it hung. 'I think I shall hang it at the office,' he said thoughtfully 'Where I can look at it more often.' She was a little disappointed, but it was true he did spend more time at the office than he did at home. He didn't give her a present but she remembered the surprise which he was no doubt keeping for this evening.

She washed her hair and paid careful attention to her makeup. She managed to get into the blue dress, whose colour John had once said had matched the colour of her eyes, she was pleased with her appearance. The evening went off pleasurably enough, John gave her flowers, freesias which she had had in her wedding bouquet, but there was still no surprise. No doubt he would give it to her when they were alone.

On their return home, John put away the car and Nicola and Julia went straight up to bed. John went up to say good night to the girls while she went into the kitchen to make coffee.

When he came downstairs he had a suitcase with him. For a moment her heart froze inside her. She fought the panic that gripped her.

'You have something to tell me,' she said 'you're leaving?'

'Yes.' He answered quietly. So quietly that her whole body was taut with anticipation.

'I'm so sorry darling' he said 'Honestly I do still love you but while you were in the States Claire and I fell in love and we have decided to live together.'

She remained outwardly calm but inside her head she shouted 'If you still love me why are you leaving?'

She hadn't meant to cry but her tears fell and dripped into her coffee. Well, now she knew what the surprise was.

A Gentle Reminder

by

Margaret Gane

'Now I know how Alice felt when she fell down the rabbit hole,' Maddie mused.

She was sure she was dreaming for she sensed that everything around her was swirling, reeling, blown gently but persistently on a stream of warm air. She wasn't sure if she was falling or merely lying still as everything around her moved. She was sure of one thing - her feet were nowhere near the ground. It must be a dream. In fact, she would be quite relieved when she awoke to the comfort of familiar surroundings.

Through the swirling haze she began to identify people. She glimpsed familiar faces from the past. There was Mrs Castle, the neighbour who had come in when she went into labour with her first child, and there was Mrs White, next-door-neighbour when she was a child living in the friendly row of terraced houses.

The movement in her 'dream' was subsiding. She was now standing in a bright street, a busy thoroughfare, yet nobody seemed to be in a hurry or doing anything in particular.

Suddenly Maddie heard her name.

'Why, there's our Maddie.'

The voice sounded familiar and Maddie turned to find her mother and father just a few yards behind her.

'Welcome, my dear, you'll like it here.' Her mother's voice was as soothing and comforting as she had always known it to be.

For some obscure reason Maddie felt unable to reply to her mother's welcome, nor to conceive what she meant by 'here'.

'I'll wake up in a minute,' she consoled herself, 'I've got a busy day ahead of me so I'll need to be up early.'

She had promised to clean Gerald's flat. He was her bachelor son who lived close by and he mentioned he was having a few friends round that evening. She just knew the flat would be in the usual mess.

But what was the time? Where was the clock? She began to panic. Not only was the clock missing but she just couldn't seem to extricate herself from this dream.

Her father's voice pierced her thoughts.

'It's good to see you, love. We've been waiting for you for such a long time.'

Maddie tried to concentrate on the words being uttered with such familiar love and tenderness. 'Waiting for you....' What on earth did they mean? And why was she talking to her mother and father. Hadn't they been dead for a good many years?

'Don't look so puzzled.' It was her mother speaking now. She obviously understood Maddie's bewilderment. 'Most people take a while to adjust but you'll like it here. Everybody does.'

'But, but, where am I?' Maddie stuttered.

'Why, this is the 'next world'. Some call it 'heaven',' her mother replied quite cheerfully and with a hint of incredulity at Maddie's apparent lack of ability to grasp the situation.

'Am I d.....?' Maddie took some time to pluck up courage to ask the question. 'Am I dead?' she eventually queried.

'Yes my dear,' mum replied. 'Some people prefer to say you have 'passed over'. Death seems so final to most people. But, as you will see it is merely a transition to another, better world.'

Maddie gasped and was ready to panic, but Dad reassured her.

'It happens to all of us sooner or later,' he sighed. 'It's a pity people dread the event. If only they would resign themselves to the inevitable they would accept it more readily. In fact, it can be a very happy experience. It's a pity we can only enjoy it once,' he mused.

'But I've still got so much to do.' Maddie spluttered. 'There's Gerald's flat to clean and I need to go up to Trevor's next weekend to see the grandchildren. Then there's Gerald's washing and ironing to return. I said I'd take it back today when I went to clean the flat. He's got no clean shirt for work tomorrow.'

'Hush, hush.' Her mother's voice was as comforting as when she had reassured her during her childhood fears.

'Don't worry. Stop fretting, lass,' her father interjected. 'Relax and enjoy yourself. Just you see how well people can cope without you.'

Maddie took her father's arm. The street faded and they were in Gerald's flat. He was in pyjamas standing in front of the open wardrobe, scratching his head.

'There, I told you', gasped Maddie, 'he's looking for a clean shirt.'

Her father attempted to reassure her, 'come now, you know how resourceful he is, he'll find something to wear.' Sure enough Gerald selected a blue and white striped shirt.

'See, that's that problem solved,' remonstrated Dad. 'You're not indispensable, my girl.'

Maddie had to agree.

'But what about his friends coming round tonight?' Just look at the state of this place.'

'Don't worry,' replied her father, 'they won't be coming.'

'But why?' questioned Maddie.

'Just wait and see,' was the reply.

The desperate need for a clean shirt prompted Gerald to visit Maddie's house during his lunch hour. He thought it strange that she wasn't in. He used his key to enter and went upstairs to the spare room where his laundry was usually left awaiting collection.

Although he knew not what prompted him, Gerald glanced into his mother's room. She was still in bed. With a usual quip about laziness he moved closer. It was obvious, without so much as a touch of the body, that she was dead. Although never being one to display his emotions, Gerald couldn't suppress a gasp, nor the overwhelming feeling of sadness which brought tears, just momentarily, to his eyes.

His levelheadedness catapulted him into action. He went to the telephone, rang the doctor, his brother and sister, and his boss at work.

The afternoon passed in a haze of frantic comings and goings. It was obvious that his mother had died in her sleep from a heart attack.

'A very peaceful way to go,' the doctor had assured him.

By the evening Gerald had made all the immediate arrangements, cancelled his evening with friends and prepared for the arrival of his brother and sister.

Maddie began to accept the fact that she was dead. The next time she ventured a glimpse of the world she had left behind so abruptly, was some weeks after her funeral. With her mother and father she returned to Gerald's flat. What a change. It was incredibly clean and tidy but it was so cold, so dark and quiet. An unshaven, sad-looking Gerald sat apparently reading but it was evident that the book he held in his hand had long since yielded its attraction.

'Why is he in such a mood?' Maddie queried.

'It's what they call 'grieving', ' explained her mother. 'He misses you. Where his sister could have a good cry and get it out of her system and his brother had his own family to return to, Gerald finds it difficult to adjust. He misses your nagging about the state of his flat. He misses you more than he will admit.'

Maddie thought for a moment then became furious.

'I told him not to mourn for me. He never would listen. Well, I'll make him listen this time.'

She walked, or rather drifted, to the corner of the room near the electrical socket into which she usually plugged her cleaner. She took out the plug. That would ensure that the clock on the video stopped and, should he be in the process of recording a programme, that would stop too. She had done it, quite innocently, so many times before and suffered Gerald's wrath as a consequence.

Next she passed close to the small radiator. The casing was loose. So many times she had knocked it off when dusting and been unable to replace it. Now it fell to the floor with quite a crash. Gerald sprang up and stood puzzling as to why the casing had fallen off. He spent the next five minutes engaged in the delicate task of reinstating it. His eye caught sight of the video recorder. The clock had stopped. The plug was out of the socket. He couldn't recall doing that.

Still puzzling he idly turned to the television. He switched it on only to find that the volume was raised to its maximum - as loud as he used to have it before... before.....

'That's it,' he mused, 'she's back. I suppose she is trying to tell me something.'

He looked round the empty room. Somehow it didn't seem as cold as previously. He turned the television off, but still it didn't seem unduly quiet. He couldn't see Maddie but he felt her presence.

'O.K. O.K. I give in.' Gerald held his hands in the air in a attitude of capitulation. 'I do miss you but I won't grieve any more. I will get on with my life.'

And then, knowing his mother would expect a rude remark, he added, 'Free from your nagging.'

A Sunday Encounter

by

Alex Whelton

The steam escaped from the two cars as they appeared to be embracing each other. Indeed, the vapour could have been construed as a result of the two autos having their first kiss. Fortunately, neither of the two drivers were injured, just shaken and perhaps somewhat angry. The man who had been driving the red sports car, strode towards the driver of the other car. His anger abated however when he espied the other driver.

She certainly was a stunner! He helped her out of the damaged saloon.

'I say, are you alright?' he asked. She looked at him, her eyes ablaze with fury, but accepted his helping hands. For a while no words were spoken, both drivers simply looked at the damaged vehicles hissing merrily away. They knew that today, of all days, recriminations would be futile. The leggy blonde had already witnessed a few cars colliding into each other.

'I suppose it was inevitable,' she said rather wearily, 'I have already seen a few irate drivers this morning. Somehow, on a quiet Sunday morning, I assumed it would be safe to venture out!'

'Me too!' he replied rather sheepishly, 'I'm afraid I did not see you in time as I turned the corner. Are you sure you're alright?'

'Just my pride mainly. My poor car, it's just a month old!'

He walked around the crashed cars to assess the damage. Her car had survived the better of the two. His low slung sports car was more crumpled. He returned to her side. 'I suppose these days they make the cars more for safety, thank goodness.' Just then, they heard another bang as two more cars collided at the opposite corner.

They looked at each other and a faint smile appeared on both their faces.

'Well,' she said,' we were told to drive extra careful today, so perhaps the many collisions that will probably occur will be as light as ours!' He glanced at his battered sports car, the hissing was slowly subsiding, even so, he knew it was beyond driving, this was definitely a job for the break down truck.

'I expect the repair garages will be having a field day today,' he said, 'although I think your car can be driven.'

Suddenly, perhaps more in apparent relief they smiled more benignly to each other. He held his hand out to her,

'Once again, I'm sorry about the collision, but, on the good side, at least I have met the lady of my dreams! My name is Tom Fisher.'

She smiled, tossed her hair back with a nod of her head. 'I expect we can always blame the government, can't we? I'm Suzy.'

They both noticed that the two irate drivers of the other crash were arguing furiously. Both Suzy and Tom were aware of other cars horns hooting angrily away in the distance.

'Oh dear!' said Suzy, 'I think I would rather be away from all this mayhem. If your car is not mobile, perhaps I could drop you off somewhere?'

By now, Tom was so entranced with this beauty before him, that his mind was racing ahead in order to think of an apt answer.

'Well, I do have a mobile phone in the car, I think I should arrange for a rescue truck first.'

Tom retrieved his phone, relieved to find it in order. He waited ages for the motoring organisation to reply, but at least they did, which was something on this day of all days.

Suzy returned to her car and tried to start the engine. The click of the switch was all that happened. Tom, by now standing beside her car, was inwardly pleased that he would have this delectable company a little longer.

'Oh dear,' he said, 'what a shame! Shall I ring again and ask for a double rescue?' He was pleased that she wouldn't be driving away, perhaps out of his life.

'That would be nice of you,' replied Suzy.

With duty done, Tom turned his attentions to Suzy who was sitting calmly in her car. She waved a hand in the direction of the passenger seat. Tom didn't need telling twice.

'They will not be here for quite a while,' he said, 'but at least they have promised us a lift to our homes.'

Police sirens sounded in the distance; this day would go down in history for the British motorist. It had been two years since the channel tunnel had been in operation, even though the inauguration had been delayed for a year, it was becoming obvious that the British motorist would change to the continental side for driving. A snap referendum had been made and the verdict resulted in the necessary bill being rushed through parliament.

It wasn't a surprise verdict really, for the majority of drivers travelled abroad with their cars more than their forefathers dared to have committed themselves to! It had been decided that some of the British drivers, with cars only four years old or less, would be allowed to use the roads in this special Sunday. Of course, most would be worry free about it, due to their driving abroad.

Unfortunately for Suzy, her experience of driving had only been to the left hand side of the road. No doubt, others, would have a memory lapse.

'I do feel rather foolish,' she said, 'I don't know what made me suddenly change to the left hand side. Possibly because I meant to turn left at the corner! Oh! I don't know, it is all rather upsetting.'

'Don't worry yourself,' said Tom sympathetically, 'we've all had to pay the special insurance premium, so, no worry there. After all, we are not injured, are we?'

She looked at him for quite a while. 'How kind of you, you have every reason to be cross,' she said.

'Not at all,' he replied, 'perhaps fate had a hand in the situation!'

Suzy looked at him, her head slightly tilted as if she did not quite understand. 'Fate?'

'Well, sort of,' replied Tom Fisher, 'I could not care less about my car, I am only too pleased to have met you.'

She tossed her hair back, as before, knowing that her crowning glory would swish around her pretty face. She looked at him, her blue eyes penetrating into his, for a while, no words were spoken.

Eventually, Tom felt that he had to break the silence. 'What do you do for a living?'

She smiled, showing perfect white teeth. Suzy still looked into his eyes. 'I'm a model. How about you?'

'As a matter of fact, I am a member of parliament. I even helped to push the bill through for traffic to drive on the right hand side of the road!'

She laughed, 'What can I say to that?'

'Well,' replied the besotted Tom, 'Perhaps you would consent to having dinner with me, maybe tonight?'

She thought hard for a while, then whispered, 'are you sure it would be only dinner?'

Tom became slightly confused for an answer, finally he blurted out, 'Well, er ... yes, only dinner, but I would like to get to know you more, truly.'

'You're so sweet! Here am I, to blame in damaging your car, and you want to get acquainted!' She placed her hand slightly over his cheek, 'Tom, I do believe you're blushing!'

He cleared his throat a little, perhaps to find the right words to say to this dream in whose car he was sitting. 'Blushing? I expect it's the heat of the moment, plus, I have never met a lady quite like you before!'

She placed a delicate forefinger over his lips. The action stalled further comments from Tom. 'We have only just met Tom. You don't really know me!'

'I don't care you are what I have always dreamed about. Will you have dinner with me, tonight, please?'

Suzy was about to reply when the jangle of the break-down trucks' chains interrupted the cosy scene.

They both alighted from her car, and watched in fascination as their two cars were winched ignominiously aboard the break-down truck.

'Okay,' said the driver, 'I'll take these to the nearest repair garage. I understand you both want a lift?'

'Yes please,' ventured Suzy. She imparted her address to the rescue driver. Tom remained silent. He didn't want to lose sight of her so soon. He just nodded in agreement. Suzy smiled sweetly at him over his action.

Inside the drivers cabin, only the news of the day was discussed, mainly the inevitable crashes. Tom was wishing the journey over, he wanted to carry on the conversation with only this vision beside him.

'Here we are then,' said the driver, 'Meyers Court.'

'Thank you so much,' said Suzy as she pressed a banknote into the driver's hand.' Thank you miss, you're very kind!'

Tom jumped out quickly, it was his chance to touch this dream once again. He had helped her to board the cabin, and now, as those elegant legs searched for the footplate, he would assist her to alight.

As they watched their two cars vanish out of sight, it was Tom who spoke first. 'It was as if they were made for each other!'

'Mm!' she replied,' the only snag is that it will affect my modelling until I can organize other transport!'

'What sort of modelling do you do?' he enquired. He couldn't take his eyes off her lovely face. She opened her hand bag and a delicate hand produced a visiting card. She smiled as she handed it to Tom.

'Here, in case you need my address for the insurance!'

He took the card and read, incredulously. 'Suzy May. Model. House visits. Phone...'

He blinked his eyes in disbelief, mouth agape, then finally found words to say.

'Does this mean, you ...er, are you, ...er' he couldn't say the right words.

'It does Tom, and you are welcome, with special rates, anytime!'

107

All that Glisters

by

Carrie Edwards

'Dear Mum, this is a picture of Jamie has done for you at Mrs Doves Nursery. It's the Snow Queen. Don't you love her crown with all its jewels stuck on! Put it on your kitchen wall and think of us when you look at it and remember it's not long till July and our visit. Love Wendy.

It had been so easy to add sparkles to Jamies picture, a little super glue was all that was needed, not even a steady hand and like all the best ideas, so simple. Even if customs opened the Jiffy bag with its happy jumble of Christmas photos, they would think nothing of it. Everyone smiling round the tree, blissfully unaware of how soon Trev would be taken from them. Among the prints were letters to Granny and other bits or artwork from Playschool. Most unlikely to attract any attention, much more likely Customs would be very interested in the blond and glamourous wife of someone doing time for a jewel robbery. Especially as she was off to stay with her Mother overseas. A Mother now married to a man of stainless character. Totally above suspicion, Thank Heavens!

There was no chance at all of selling the gems here. You always needed explanations of where things had come from, proof of ownership, receipts, etc. The police circulated particulars of missing items, honest dealers were reluctant to touch anything 'not kosher'. Someone not quite straight would buy them but only at a fraction of what they were worth. Then you had the worry they might not keep their mouth shut. They might get greedy and want more worse still, tell the tale over a drink or two of how stones from a famous theft had passed through their hands - and as Wendy and God know, walls have ears. Of course you can cut stones down but once you start cutting you cut profits as well. Wendy had no intention of doing that, she wanted every last penny. The prison sentence was the price to be paid. They wouldn't pay that and lose out on the rewards. *No Way Jose!*

Where Mum lived it was a different story. People didn't ask so many questions. And prices were higher. Much more satisfactory. Lots of not quite squeaky clean folk had 'retired' there. Outside the reach of the long arm of the law. Enjoying a lovely climate and a good living. Always keen to make a swift buck but best of all, not too nosey.

Betty delighted as ever top see an English stamp, bent to pick up the package. She would make a cup of coffee for her and Bill then they could savour the news from home and enjoy the view from the terrace.

The rocky peaks were clad in firs and reached out it seemed for the clear blue sky. A few bright orange roofed cottages clung to the sides of the slopes. Here and there vineyards, looking from a distance like squares of ribbed knitting with their dead straight rows of grapes. It was a vista hard to get tired of. The edge of the terrace was lined with big terracotta pots of geraniums, Betty's pride and joy. She missed Wendy terribly and worried so much about her and the two little boys. Even more so now Trev was in prison. Money did not seem to be a problem, Trev had seen to it that if ever the worst happened there was something to see Wendy through (in the manner to which she had very happily become accustomed). Still she was so young to be bringing up the boys on her own. No doubt she had to put up with gossip and snide comments in a posh neighbourhood like that.

They were thrilled with Jamies pictures. Betty fixed them to the door of the fridge freezer with her collection of novelty magnets. Fat little owls and Penguins who looked down their beaks. Pride of place for the work of Granny's favourite little boy. To be admired daily and to be seen by Jamie himself when he came for his holiday in the summer.

Accidents always happen quickly and afterwards no-one can ever quite remember what they did. Bill was up on the steps, touching up a little mark on the kitchen wall, paint can on a hook, brush in hand, miles away in thought when Betty spoke. He turned to hear what she said and must have over balanced. Seconds later he was flat on his back on the cold stone tiles. Lovely and cool in the heat of the summer but a very unsympathetic landing place for an overweight middle aged man!

Doctor was summoned. He made the long journey up the cream ribbon road that wound round the mountain. No broken bones but straight to bed on a board for that back, if trouble was to be avoided. Bill happily crept off for a weeks rest, pleased that Betty had to clear the awful mess and not him.

Betty looked around in disbelief, could a pot of paint really have spread that far. Everything seemed to have been touched by the spreading white lake. The floor, the windows and blinds, the cooker and the fridge freezer, nothing had escaped. Where did she start? Bits and pieces not moved for such a small job could go straight in the bin. She had better things to do than try to clean them up. Jamie's picture too. Such a shame. When the Children had phoned last month to wish her 'Happy Birthday' she had thanked them for the pictures and promised they would see them all on display in Granny's kitchen when they came to stay. Betty could not save the picture but she could replace it! Jamie at only four years old would not remember the details. She would do a copy. She had lots of old costume jewelry she would happily break up and stick on queenies crown. Anything to please her favourite little boy, he would never know the difference!

A Very Brief Encounter

by

Simon Croft

In a rather long life, I have rarely experienced such a fog as the one which enveloped the old railway station that winter's evening and I, frankly, was chilled to the bone.

The wait for the train seemed interminable and it wasn't all that long before my imagination began to work overtime.

In situations like this, different stories of various kinds come to mind and this night was so dark and mysterious that, I am sure, *anyone* would have imagined the most dreadful things!

Somewhere in the distance an Owl hooted mournfully - and I didn't blame it for feeling melancholy.

This was farming country, so that I shouldn't have found it a bit unusual to hear a cow mooing somewhere - and I wasn't - but what *did* surprise me, was that the lowing seemed to be coming from, of all places, the station platform!

Thinking that a cow must have escaped from a nearby farm, I went to the door of the waiting room and looked out - which was a bit stupid of me, because it was impossible to see anything which was more than a yard in front of me - but look I did ... and saw nothing.

'Go and sit down, you idiot!' I told myself, 'you're letting the fog in and it's cold!' So I shut the door and went back to sit beside the miserable little fire which tried to glow in the waiting room's fireplace.

Hardly had I settled down as close to the fireplace as possible, when I heard the distant, dolorous sound of a train whistle in the distance ... and, somehow, I had the feeling that even the old train hated being out on a night like this.

Rather thankfully I gathered up my luggage, left the waiting room and went to stand out on the platform, where I waited for the train to arrive, which it did - about five minutes later.

It crawled into the station and came to a stop with a clanking of buffers followed by the voice of the Guard announcing the name of the station... but his voice was muffled by the fog.

Entering a dimly lit compartment, I put my luggage up on the rack, closed the carriage door and sat down, pulling my overcoat close about me to keep in some warmth.

It was not until I was seated that I realised that I was not alone in the compartment.

Sitting on the other side was a gentleman muffled - just as I was - in a warm greatcoat, suede gloves and a warm velour hat.

'Good evening,' I said, 'although it's not really a very *nice* evening is it?'

My companion lowered his newspaper and smiled, 'No,' he answered, 'I do agree, it is a most unpleasant evening.'

'I shouldn't think that anyone would travel on a night like this,' I said, 'unless he had to... and, unfortunately, I have to.'

He smiled again and said, 'Once again, I agree with you. I too have to travel tonight, just as I have done for the last thirty-five years.'

I whistled softly, 'Thirty-five years,' I said, 'not *every* night, surely?'

He nodded, 'Yes,' he replied, 'every night, each and every night, same train, same compartment, Summer and Winter.'

I shook my head in sympathy, smiled and said, 'You must enjoy the journey, but I can't say that I do!'

My companion shook his head and answered, 'You would think so, wouldn't you?' He folded his newspaper and laid it on the seat beside him, then went on, 'but I don't... I hate it!'

Thinking to myself that this might be a good time to change the subject, I said, 'You know, a night such as this sets a fertile imagination working.'

He nodded and said, 'Yet again, I find that I must agree with you, but - in my case - imagination is almost non-existent and so... I am quite safe, you see.'

I laughed outright, 'I think that, on a night like this, imagination would have to be *completely* non-existent, not 'almost'!'

He shrugged and answered, 'I don't believe in Fairies, Witches or Hobgoblins, so that I can repeat, I am perfectly safe.'

Settling back more comfortably, I asked, 'Would it be an impertinence if I were to ask you what you do?'

'Do?' He repeated.

'Yes,' I said, 'are you a Business man, or an Artist, or - or a Doctor... or what?'

'Oh, I see,' he replied, 'no, I am neither of those things, nowadays I 'do' nothing.'

That took me aback, so I asked, 'Forgive my persistence, but if you - as you say - do nothing,' I rubbed my chin in thought, 'why do you travel on this train - especially on a night such as this?'

'You *are* persistent,' he gave me a wry sort of smile, 'but I suppose that your question is a natural one.'

I waited for a second or two, expecting him to go on and tell me about his occupation... he wasn't a Business man, an Artist nor a Doctor, so what was he?

Since he gave no sign of continuing, I said, 'Well, you've got me intrigued, so what are you and why do you travel on this train - as you say - every night?'

He looked at me - almost staring - for a full minute, then spoke, 'Do you *really* want to know?' He asked.

I nodded and answered,

'You've definitely got me interested... yes, I *really* want to know!'

He sighed and shook his head as if he couldn't believe that I *was* interested, then he looked unblinkingly at me again and nodded to himself.

'Very well,' he said, 'you obviously *are* interested, so perhaps I'd better tell you.'

As I settled back in the seat again, he went on, 'Thirty-five years ago, a murder took place,' he waved a hand around the compartment, then went on, 'here, on this train, in this very compartment!'

'Thirty-five years ago?' I asked.

He nodded, 'yes... in fact, tonight is the thirty-fifth anniversary.'

Shivering a little in my greatcoat, I remarked, 'Wow! This really *is* a story!'

He nodded again and said, 'Yes... it's almost a horror story, because I was here - in this compartment - on that night... and I've been here ever since!'

When the full import of what he had just said penetrated what I was using for brains at that moment, I said, *'You've been here ever since that night?!'*

Yet again he nodded and said, 'Every minute of 'ever since' and it's been an awfully long time, believe me!'

At last I was beginning to *think,* so I said, 'Now, wait a minute!... If you've been here ever since... that means that... that you... that means that you are... '

'Yes?' My companion prompted me.

By now, I was struggling against the turmoil in my mind, but I responded to the prompting and said, 'That means that you are... you are a... a... a ghost!'

He smiled, 'There,' he said, 'that wasn't so difficult to say, was it?'

But I was intending to complete my train (?) of thought, so I went on, 'You were murdered here and now you have to ride on this train to... to... to the end of time?!'

To my surprise, he smiled again, but shook his head, 'You are *almost* right,' he told me, 'except for one or two small details - I *was* condemned to ride this train, but only until I found someone who would listen to my story... and believe it.'

Because I was intrigued, I asked, 'What details were wrong?'

This time the smile which he gave me was decidedly wry as he shrugged.

'Just small ones... *I* was not the victim,' he said, 'I was the murderer... I used a gun... but the bullet ricocheted and killed *me* too... now I must move on to another destination... the Nether Regions *do* exist, you know!'

He shrugged once more, shook his head, then smiled at me and added, 'But thank you very much for listening to my story... and I have the strongest feeling that you *do* believe it?'

Giving him a quizzical look, I nodded and answered, 'You know, it may sound... unbelievable, but never-the-less... I *do* believe it!'

He gave me another straight look, then smiled, 'Yes,' he said, 'you *do* believe me... thank you again... and now the time has come for me to bid you, 'Goodbye'.'

And with that, he rose, gave me a small bow - and vanished... which is why I am now in possession of a thirty-five year old newspaper bearing the front page headline:

'Killer and victim slain - by the same bullet!'

The Girl in Brown

by

W Elliott

I was an only child, and when my parents were killed in a train accident I became the ward of Great-Aunt Emily. She was not fond of young people, and had consequently seen little of my father and nothing of me.

She made certain that the boarding school I attended was a reputable establishment, paid extra for me to stay there during the holidays, and had a standing order with her local bookshop for a suitable volume to be despatched for my birthday and at Christmas.

Her duty done, and her conscience clear, she had no need for further concern.

I was a lonely child, having little in common with the other girls at school. All of them had families or at least someone who cared about them. They all thought me rather odd, and none of them could understand the need I had for affection.

The Headmistress was an austere, scholarly woman, never likely to inspire warm feelings, and the English mistress, whose kindness, and perhaps pity, might have begun to fill the gap in my life, left after only one term to marry a missionary in West Africa.

I withdrew into myself and kept my own company. Desperately in need of friends, I invented them. Naturally enough, I suppose, with my bereavement and the indifference of Great-Aunt Emily, they were fantastic and often tragic figures, owing much to the books I had read.

I was the only girl at school during the Christmas holidays. The duty mistress was the science teacher, an intense, ambitious woman, whose only reason for volunteering to stay on at school was the continuation of her current piece of research, which kept her in the laboratory from early morning until late at night. I was left completely to my own resources.

Tired of remote heroines, I invented the girl in brown. At first I could see her only in the distance, or disappearing around corners ahead of me, but gradually she came closer, and sometimes she followed me into the garden or sat at the table when I ate.

I did not have a name for her. She never spoke and she never acknowledged my presence. I accepted this and did not think it at all extraordinary. It was enough that she was there, and I was no longer alone.

She was a pretty girl, with a round rosy face, and fat golden plaits tied with brown ribbons. The dress she wore was brown too, long and old-fashioned, just like those worn by the girls in the class pictures hanging in the entrance hall dating from the founding of the school nearly fifty years ago.

She sat with me at breakfast on Christmas morning, opposite the science mistress, who was engrossed in her latest notes. I opened the parcel from my Great-Aunt's bookshop. This year they had sent me 'David Copperfield', the binding matching the 'Domby and Son' of my birthday and 'Pickwick Papers' of last Christmas.

I excused myself from the table, but the science mistress did not even hear. I took my book to the dormitory, where all the other beds had been stripped, and put it in my box at the foot of my bed.

The girl in brown had come with me, skipping up the stairs in a complicated routine that involved missing every third step.

I looked through the window. The sky was leaden, and a few feathers of snow were beginning to float down. I put on my coat and picked up my scarf. Before it became too cold I would go into the orchard, which was out of bounds, and perhaps climb the pear tree in the far corner. The girl in brown could come with me. I thought she would enjoy breaking what seemed such a silly school rule.

I left the dormitory and went down to the hall. The girl in brown was on the landing, playing a sort of hopscotch in the squared pattern of the ancient linoleum. Still standing on one leg, she began to hop down the stairs, her plaits flopping on her shoulders. On the third stair she over-balanced.

Her eyes bulging with fear, and her mouth gaping soundlessly, down she fell, tumbling over and over, into a dishevelled heap of arms and legs at my feet. There was blood on her forehead, and her eyes were open and staring in horror.

I heard the sound of screaming. It grew louder and louder, until my throat was raw with it, and I knew that it was I who screamed.

I had to get away from those awful staring eyes, and I ran through the door and out into the orchard. I stumbled over a branch hidden beneath the long grass and fell heavily. There was a terrible pain in my head, and I felt sick.

I remembered no more until I awoke in my bed. It was very quiet and dark except for a shaded lamp on the table. The science mistress was seated on a

116

chair, reading her inevitable notes. The door opened and the housekeeper came in with a steaming mug.

'Is there any change?' she whispered.

I tried to speak, but no words came. The science mistress accepted the mug gratefully.

'No,' she said. 'She is very restless, but has not regained consciousness.'

The housekeeper clucked sympathetically. 'Poor child. Let's hope it isn't pneumonia like the doctor fears. Though it'll hardly be surprising, what with her lying out in the snow for goodness knows how long. It's a mercy she was found at all.'

She pulled the coverlet up to my chin and tucked the blanket in tightly. I tried to tell her that I was already too hot, but she took no notice. Shaking her head, she left the science mistress to her notes and her cocoa. I drifted off into sleep.

When I awoke again it was daylight, with that peculiar brightness that comes only from reflected snow.

It was icy cold. I felt very strange and rather dizzy. Gradually the muzziness passed, and I could see that the science mistress had gone, and the housekeeper was sitting in the chair, dozing.

There was a girl lying in the bed. She was unnaturally still, her hair lank on the pillow, her shadowed eyes closed, and her face waxen white. She looked strangely familiar, but I could not quite place her.

I heard a giggle behind me, and there was the girl in brown. For the first time she spoke to me.

'My name's Mary,' she said. 'I'm so glad you've come. I've been waiting such a long time.' She took my hand, and a warm glow seemed to spread through me.

'Come on,' she said. 'It's a beautiful day. Let's go into the orchard and I'll show you the squirrel's nest in the pear tree. There are three babies there, and if you're very gentle they'll let you stroke them.'

We went out of the dormitory, away from the pale cold figure in the bed. We went down the stairs, past all the old class photographs, and out through the door.

The sun was shining, the birds were singing, and the air was full of the perfume of spring flowers. The grass felt good under my bare feet. I kilted my nightdress round my waist so that I could keep up with the girl in brown.

We ran laughing through trees laden with blossoms like snow. I was happier than I had ever been in my life.

117

Special Issue

by

Phillip Murrell

The special edition postage stamp had been issued to celebrate the 150th anniversary of Rowland Hill's Penny Post system of 1840, and on it, a river was depicted running across its middle ground. Since no weir or waterfall or other tell-tale sign was in evidence, the direction of its flow could only be guessed at. Even the river's width was difficult to estimate on account of what must have been the somewhat lowly position of the camera's eye. In the background could be seen hills. Not the huge, straddling, marching-onward hills of, say, Northumbria, but lesser hills that spoke more of Hampshire or Kent. The scene could have been almost any one of a number of locations. The photographer had done an excellent job in preserving its geographical anonymity. A man in a silver grey suit occupied the foreground and had been skilfully superimposed against this idyllic, if elusive, back-drop. He was shown striding purposefully into the picture bearing a letter, which, though tilted slightly from the horizontal, faced out, square-on to the viewer. The man's face could not be seen since the stamp's designer had shown only the central portion of his person. There was a certain attractive charm, a strangeness almost, to what at first appeared an unremarkable enough little scene. However, everything about this picture contrived to rivet one's attention to the letter the man carried. Affixed to this letter could be detected a tiny stamp. This stamp within a stamp, now not more than three millimetres across, faithfully reproduced in exquisite detail the precise situation which surrounded it: the river, the rolling hills, the truncated silver grey suited man hurrying with a letter - a letter on which could be seen, just, a yet smaller stamp.

Reginald Manning a philatelist and retired platemaker living in the Welsh marches was astonished at the exceptional quality of this commemorative issue.

'Hm,' he muttered to himself, smoothing his neatly trimmed moustache, 'a stamp on a stamp is one thing, but a stamp on a stamp on a stamp... well, this almost defies credibility.'

Bringing down his wire-framed spectacles from his broad forehead where he was wont sometimes to park them to the more familiar position on the bridge

118

of his nose, he arose, crossed the book-lined study and ascended the stairs to the landing. The tortoise-shell handled magnifying glass he had been using was simply not powerful enough to show the stamp's intricate detail and so his father's old brass microscope was retrieved from the attic and pressed into service.

Carefully drawing the image into focus, the first stamp, the three millimetre one, was revealed. And yes, even the tiniest of addresses had been copied in minute detail: 5 High Street, Anytown, AN1 2TN.

'No prizes for originality there,' thought Mr Manning with mounting excitement. 'Oh, the thrill of it!' He could hardly contain his elation.

'Tea. I must have a cup of tea,' he exclaimed aloud, momentarily clasping his hands together as he did so. Then, feeling as though he were on a cloud, strode off towards the kitchen.

Mr Manning liked tea and kept a small collection of various types ranged along the top shelf of his polished oak dresser; Ceylon, English breakfast, Lapsang Souchong and, for special occasions, Earl Grey. Today it would be the Earl Grey. He also enjoyed opera and hummed 'La mia Dorabella' from 'Cosi fan tutte' as he busied himself with his tea-making. Soon all was ready. The tea in the pot, drawing, the little bowl of sugar, the milk jug, the cup, the saucer, teaspoon and strainer and, feeling in a somewhat celebratory mood, two chocolate digestives. He always gave his tummy a couple of pats when awarding himself such treats and did not fail to do so on this occasion. Finally, he placed all the tea paraphernalia carefully - reverently almost - on a white linen covered rectangular tray.

Back at his desk and with tea poured Mr Manning resumed his position over the microscope.

'Now for the tiniest one of all - the third one.' His trembling fingers moved the glass specimen plate holding the stamp into the field of vision, and suddenly there it was! It was a miracle! But, 'Hello,' thought Mr Manning, 'what's this?' Gone was the Anytown address and in its place in minuscule characters were just two mono-syllabic words, the second of which read: *Off.*

Mr Manning turned puce with rage. He had been insulted beyond words.

Reaching angrily for a pen and writing paper a strong letter of complaint was soon underway to the Postmaster General concerning the discovery of the four-letter word. Pulling out a little drawer in his writing bureau he took out a stamp, ironically another offending one. He hesitated for a moment, frowned even deeper, then placed the stamp firmly on the envelope, bringing the side of

119

his fist down upon it with a force sufficient enough to cause the china on the tray to rattle and send a brief shiver across the membranous surface of his tea.

Leaving his cottage, he crossed the little stone bridge spanning the river and began the short walk to the nearby pillar-box. Though rain had washed the village streets earlier in the day the sun shone bravely out from a growing patch of blue, lighting up the surrounding hills.

We leave Reginald Manning hurrying off into the distance, assiduously avoiding the puddles of rain, ever mindful of splashing his neatly pressed silver grey suit or of dropping the letter he holds by his side.

Blooming Cheek

by

Rosemary Rogan

Rachel stood by the window gazing out at her unruly garden. Yet in spite of the weeds it was full of colour and Rachel liked it as it was. What if the lawn did need mowing and the roses weren't pruned, she had every intention of relaxing in a deck chair beside the rambling rose that now occupied more and more of the garden. She could see Cumro already out there, sniffing round the roots, searching for objects long since buried and now to be dug up again. His short tail quivered in anticipation as he scrabbled about in the soft earth.

Vague feelings of guilt marred Rachel's pleasure in the idyllic day. Few people understood her relief at being on her own. It wasn't the memory of David's death that upset her, merely the circumstances of it.

There had been a time when she'd idolized David. She'd met him when she became his receptionist. She'd been amazed and impressed by how a few minutes chat with him made such a difference to his many adoring patients. Everyone thought highly of him, so it wasn't surprising that Rachel, young and impressionable as she was, thought so too.

David was everything she was not. He was confident, talkative and capable. Rachel had spent her life coping with a mother who was irritable and unreasonable. She failed to see that David's charm merely covered up a selfish and flawed personality.

She remembered that first evening. The evening Surgery had run overtime, and she'd panicked at missing the last bus.

'Not to worry,' David said breezily, 'I've got one late visit to do, then I'll deliver you back safe and sound to your Mum's waiting arms.' Twenty years older than her, he made her sound terribly unsophisticated.

'I wouldn't ever go home,' she blurted out, 'if I had anywhere else to go.'

They reached a beauty spot, a lake that had once been an ancient shrine. It was late summer and large greenish brown leaves swirled on the surface of the water. Mystery was in the air. Rachel wished, for everyone said that this lake granted wishes. David stopped the car and they sat in silence.

'Why did you say that about not going home?' He asked, yet when Rachel began to explain he cut her short and covered her face with kisses. He kissed

121

her in a masterful, yet curiously impersonal way, almost as though performing a medical operation.

Rachel, who'd never been kissed by a real man before, murmured 'she thought she'd better go home else Mum might be angry.'

Yet she was thrilled, feeling both excited and flattered. David's lips moved against her ear, telling her not to worry about the old crow. She giggled, and gave herself up to the enjoyment of the minute.

Not long after, David proposed. Rachel wondered whether this was the result of her plea to the ancient lake. Her mother, who so often grumbled at her presence now became furiously jealous and so when David pressed her to make up her mind quickly, she did. She hid her disappointment at finding that their honeymoon was to be spent at a medical conference.

Rachel soon discovered that her popular husband was as much a tyrant at home as her mother had been. But the greatest blow was finding that he had no intention of having a family.

'I've had all that,' he told her shortly, 'and I can tell you, it's not worth it.' He re-iterated the necessity of making sure she didn't become pregnant by mistake. His previous marriage had ended in divorce and neither his children or his former wife were ever mentioned. Sadly, Rachel lavished love on Cumro, the small dog she insisted on having, saying that a guard dog was a necessity to protect their property.

David seemed devoid of personal emotion, perhaps because he gave too much of himself in his professional life. The only thing he was passionate about was his garden. His lawn was as smooth and perfect as a bowling green. Passers-by, peering through the white wooden gate, marvelled at the lines of tulips, red hot pokers and cool blue irises that stood straight and proud. All David's flowers were tall and held themselves erect.

The only exception was a rambling rose. This dominated one corner of the garden. David talked often of uprooting it, despite Rachel's disapproval. Cumro was forbidden to set paw on the lawn. Instead, he and Rachel took long rambling walks through the woods at the back of the house.

As the rose grew bigger and wilder so did David's dislike of it. As if to spite him it often gave shelter to Cumro when he was in trouble. Of all the flowers in the garden only the rose seemed to have a free spirit, and because of that, Rachel loved it.

One day David marched into the garden with a grimmer than usual expression on his face and a pair of bright green gardening gloves in his hands. Rachel stayed inside, though she flattened her nose against the window. Hardly aware of what she was doing she moved her lips in prayer,

'Lord, save the rose, don't let him hurt it.' Later, when she recalled that prayer she felt uneasy, for amazingly, it was answered!

It was weird. It was as if the rose, rudely attacked, decided to fight back. One minute David was hacking at it with an axe and the next he was embroiled helplessly within its lethal thorns. He cried out, but only slowly did Rachel go to his aid. Bright red blood oozed from a number of savage scratches.

Excitedly, Cumro sunk his teeth into his master's helpless leg. Rachel was powerless to free her imprisoned husband. The sun beat down and David's face became redder and redder. At first he thrashed about, trying to free his arms from his old jacket. Then, just as a neighbour appeared, he gave a shuddering jerk and collapsed in a lifeless heap.

Cumro started to whine, and then the rose seemed to voluntarily withdraw its talons. David lay spreadeagled on his perfect lawn. A magpie cocked its head in a nearby tree, staring with an indifferent eye.

David was buried in the local cemetery and the whole village turned out to bid farewell to such a popular figure.

The villagers often remarked that it was a real shame that his young widow should be so careless towards the lovely garden that her husband had left behind. Yet everyone looked with awe at the delicate wild rose that seemed to grow bigger every year.

With a sigh, Rachel dismissed the past and went out into the garden to sit in the deckchair, happy to be on her own with only the dog Cumro as a companion.

The Invitation

by

Stanley Smith

Although Sushila Naidu slept late on Sundays, she awoke early this Sunday morning - the first in Autumn - as it was a special day. She had invited her neighbour Doctor Sheila Smith, a spinster in her mid-fifties, to dinner.

Ever since she had come to live next to her on the third floor of a new block of flats in North London, she had desperately sought the Doctor's friendship. A month had elapsed since her arrival and all that had been achieved was an exchange of half smiles when she met her, without design, on the stairs.

Meanwhile, she had learned a great deal about the Doctor from their mutual cleaning lady Mrs Thompson.

'She's an ear, nose and throat specialist and works at the hospital,' confided Mrs Thompson one Saturday afternoon after completing her work in Sushila's flat. 'She's ever so fussy, you know. Has a lot of old clocks and silver. I have to be very careful dusting them. Everything in her flat has to be spic and span.' Mrs Thompson, small and rotund, paused and then remarked, 'She's generous though. Pays well and always gives me a present at Christmas.'

From these observations, Sushila could not help feeling how much the Doctor resembled her mother who lived several thousand miles away in India. They were about the same age and she remembered from her past life with her parents, how fastidious and finicky her mother had always been. Of course, it was easy for her, Sushila reminisced. Her husband was a wealthy merchant and in their home in Bombay, there were many servants. They often gave dinner parties and guests kept dropping in at all hours. Her father always maintained that the best way to gain the esteem of people was to serve them an excellent home cooked meal.

One Monday evening, after returning from work at an Estate Agents' office, Sushila met Dr Smith at the bottom of the staircase leading to their flats. They walked up the stairs together and this time, abandoning all her shyness, spoke to her and introduced herself. Before the Doctor entered her flat, Sushila asked her to come to dinner the following Sunday. Doctor Smith was surprised at the sudden invitation but accepted as she had no other engagement on that day.

'I'll make some Indian curries,' Sushila suggested. 'I hope you don't mind eating Indian food.'

'Not at all,' the Doctor replied, 'provided they are not too hot and spicy. My grandparents lived in India and they always relished their Sunday curried tiffing. I've never been to India but my mother often cooked chicken curry.'

'Good,' said Sushila. 'In our culture, the women cook. My poor husband, who died last year loved my curries. But like you, he preferred them mild. So you see Doctor, I know how to make them just right.' She then added, 'I'll come and tell you when the meal is ready.'

All through the week, Sushila did not meet Dr Smith again. However, she never forgot their last meeting when they chatted; and now the appointed day had arrived when they would share a meal - an auspicious beginning to a lasting friendship - she hoped. For starters, she decided on serving small pieces of barbecued chicken kebabs with a fresh green salad. Lamb curry with pilau rice would follow and for sweet there would be mango ice cream. All the necessary ingredients awaited her in the kitchen. The specially selected tender meat, the onions, cummin, cloves, saffron and cardamons. Of course, she was not going to use ordinary curry paste. She was going to grind all the different spices herself. Also, she would clean the rice of its impurities and then wash it, again and again till all the starch was removed. It was going to be the best meal she had ever made.

While Sushila cooked, she reflected on the years gone by. She was twenty when she had come to England in the early eighties to enter into an arranged marriage with an almost unknown bridegroom. After five years, her husband died of cancer. He was a successful accountant and was gentle and kind. She believed he loved her deeply and continued to do so despite the fact that she bore him no children. They lived in a large detached house in Surrey with his stern mother and two younger brothers.

After her husband's death, she could not continue to bear the tyranny of her mother-in-law. It was bad enough when he had been alive, but now that he was no more, life with the elder Mrs Naidu and her two spoilt sons had become unbearable. After all, she was an educated college girl and used to a certain amount of freedom in India. Here, she went nowhere. She was stuck in the house all day listening to the lamentations of her mother-in-law. She just had to get away from it all and was overjoyed when her release came.

She was offered a job in an Estate Agents' office in Hampstead. Her employer, Jack Williams, an old family friend, found her attractive and intelligent. Moreover, she spoke Hindi and had studied Arabic in Bombay. This was an asset as there were many wealthy Asians and Arabs seeking large properties in the area. The men were able to converse fluently in English, but many of their wives only spoke their own dialect.

The hours sped by. It was almost six o'clock in the evening. Sushila had finished preparing her dishes and spread them out on her favourite embroidered linen table-cloth. She wrapped her olive-skinned body in a green silk sari and wearing her favourite pieces of exotic jewellery, went to Doctor Smith's flat to tell her dinner was ready.

A few moments after she knocked, Doctor Smith came to the door dressed in a pair of blue slacks and a white pullover. Her grey eyes betrayed a look of surprise.

'Doctor Smith, please come, the dinner is ready,' advised Sushila.

'I'm sorry I can't come Mrs Naidu, I've already eaten,' the Doctor answered rather coldly.

Sushila felt confused. 'But don't you remember Doctor, I invited you for dinner today. And I said I'd come and tell you when it's ready.'

'Yes, I know you invited me to dinner,' said the Doctor a trifle firmly, 'but a Sunday dinner is usually served at mid-day. I waited till two o'clock and when you didn't call, I thought you'd forgotten; so I cooked myself some ham and eggs.'

Sushila's confusion persisted and she apologised profusely. She tried to vindicate herself. 'I was expecting you to come in the evening. That is what I meant. Oh! I know I should have come early this morning and told you.'

Her large brown eyes were full of pain and her face transformed itself into an innocent young girl's appeal. She ventured hopefully, 'I know you have eaten Doctor, but that was several hours ago. Please come and at least sample some of my dishes. They are quite tasty, you know, and I have some excellent Darjeeling tea.'

'I'm sorry Mrs Naidu, I just can't,' reiterated the Doctor. 'I never eat anything on Sunday evenings - except a piece of cheese or a few biscuits while I'm watching television. Besides, I can't leave my flat. I'm expecting a call from my niece in Australia.'

Sushila felt her world was being smashed into little pieces but she did not give up.

'Perhaps I may bring some of my dishes and tea to your flat,' she recommended. 'This way, we both can eat something and you won't miss your niece's call.'

126

Doctor Smith was thrown for a moment but she quickly regained her composure.

'No, no,' she repeated, 'that won't be necessary. And if you'll now excuse me Mrs Naidu, I'll go inside. I've got some work to attend to.' Then shrugging her shoulders she said: 'Please don't worry about what's happened. Put it down to...' she groped, 'to an unfortunate misunderstanding. Perhaps we could have a meal together some other time.'

Sushila felt like a beggar as the door closed against her. She returned to her flat and looked forlornly at the untouched dishes of food.

'What a waste!' She sighed, 'and what a blunder I have made.'

Throughout the night, Sushila hardly slept. She was haunted by the thought that all the time and effort she spent in trying to win the Doctor's friendship and affection had ended in a blaze of smoke. A feeling of despair seized her. When she did find some brief interludes of sleep, all she saw in her dream's eye was the Doctor's strong body and fine-boned face with its crown of thick hair flecked with silver. She wore a scornful look while rejecting her invitation.

Early next morning, she swallowed a cup of black coffee with a few aspirins and decided to leave immediately lest she encountered Doctor Smith outside her door. She would never be able to bear the coldness she imagined had now entered the Doctor's heart after the previous night's fiasco. The lift was out of order and descending the stairs, often two at a time, she slipped and fell. A growing darkness overcame her as she finally reached the floor.

Later, on awakening, she found herself in a strange bedroom and Doctor Smith was leaning over her. There was no ice in her expression.

'There, there, Mrs Naidu,' she whispered, 'you're all right. Just a nasty fall. I'll make you some tea.' Tears misted Sushila's eyes and placing her arms round her held her close. The Doctor responded warmly. Sushila had not felt so happy in a long, long, time.

Another Year

by

Josephine Blyth

Bob burst through the doorway of the art room, just as the bell rang.

'Hello Miss, I'm not late Miss. Have a good holiday Miss,' he said flinging the words at me across the room.

He did not wait for a reply but descended on George his mate with a heavy thump on George's back. 'OK pal,' he said. 'What in hell's name have you done to your hair,'

George looked at him in dismay. 'I've shaved the sides off, he said, 'got fed up with it, like a bush it was,' he said.

George's hair was still long and bushy, like some shaggy mountain goat. You could just see his face beneath this overgrown mane.

'I do tie it back when I work Miss I promise, but, well, today I forgot Miss,' he said reassuringly, waiting for me to complain about his tangled mop.

I looked at Bob in reply to his greeting.

'Yes, I had a good holiday, thanks for asking, and you?'

'Bit boring miss, nothing to do.'

I smiled wryly, for Bob was not renowned for his energetic application to work or play. He was often to be found sitting outside a classroom, astounded that his comments had upset the fraught member of staff. The rest of my group drifted in confidently. This had been their pastoral home for the last three years.

'Morning Miss.'

'Hi, Miss.'

'Had a good holiday Miss.'

'Glad to be back Miss.'

Tom, Brian, Lucy and Tracey briefly listening to my reply before huddling together to chat about their own holiday experiences and conquests. Within minutes the room was buzzing with the chatter of twenty-two fifteen year old boys and girls frantically catching up on the latest gossip. I passed round the new timetables and the like that had been heaped on us by Brian Matthews our Head of Year.

Several of the group muttered under their breath,

'More bits of paper to lose... '

'Miss, why do we need all this lot then?'

'So you know what is going on this term,' I said.

Strange to say but a warm glow of pleasure and contentment flowed through me. Yes, they had all arrived back safely; no casualties; they were all as they left, full of life, just a few weeks older, maybe a little more responsible now that they had reached the senior part of the school. It was good to be back in familiar surroundings with these people I had grown to love. They are such a happy, friendly group; with untold problems; needing support, and at times you could cheerfully strangle several of them, but, none-the-less, a warm, caring lot. The room buzzed with questions.

'Who have I got for Science Miss?'

'I'll have the list after lunch, Charlie.'

'Where do I go for Maths, Miss?'

'Go next door and ask Miss Jordan for the list please, Susie.'

'Can I go and see Mr Branch, I don't want to go canoeing Miss?'

'He's in L6 this term.'

'Thanks Miss.'

'Miss can I go to the toilet Miss?' I nod.

'Can I change my option Miss?'

'Go and see Mr Matthews Ralph.'

At that point Brian came in with a new boy. Simon was a tall self assured young man who would fit in well.

'Brian, can you have a chat with Ralph about his options?'

'Ralph, go with Mr Matthews now and get things sorted.'

That first hour was quite frantic, with all the to-ing and fro-ing. A busy two years lay ahead, but people like Bob and George would find it boring and frustrating. Not because they were without brains, but they have not yet learned that you cannot beat the system and those who try are thought to be misfits and trouble-makers. They had now reached the age and stage of holding hands under the desk, snatching kisses behind the teacher's back.

'Tracey, leave Tom alone, remember where you are. Not in lessons.'

'Sorry Miss, I forgot,' she replied with that wide grin of hers. Love, sex sensuality. What a wonder this miracle of life, this growth to womanhood and manhood.

'Bob, give it a rest please, let someone else have a chance to talk. You're giving me a headache already.'

'Sorry Miss. So much to say.'

129

God, I sound like Joyce Grenfell!

In the midst of this mayhem, arms are flung round my neck and a kiss plonked on my cheek. It was Alicia.

'I'm back,' she said, 'just had to come and say hello. Still at home though, Miss. Mum was so upset about me moving out, Miss. We had a long chat, Miss, and things are much better now, Miss.' All this without a breath.

'I'm glad things are well. Good to see you back.'

'Thanks Miss. Guess what Miss. My boyfriend Miss. Wants to get engaged Miss. Freaked out, didn't I Miss. Bit soon Miss, don't know him much yet do I Miss.'

'Good for you Alicia.'

She looked at me smilingly, pleased at my approval, gave me another hug and kiss and rushed off to see her friends. The bell rang, chairs scraped along the floor, a rush of feet towards the door and the room was empty. Break time at last.

'You are a wonder Frances,' I said, as she handed me a much needed cup of coffee. 'What would we do without you. All that chat. They are so full of life this morning, any chance its a full moon tonight.' I turned to Chris. 'Were yours the same?'

'Worse,' said Chris, flopping into his chair.

Another mad hour ensued before lunch time when as I walk over to the canteen I find myself humming the words of an old music hall tune, 'He married the girl with the strawberry curl and the band played on,' and laughed at myself. Has the madness of being back set in so soon. The brain is a funny thing, the way songs, words and images pop into it without bidding. That new lad seemed nice, but poor George, still as looney as ever; leaves his brain behind when he comes to school; head so full of music; such a dreamer, always saying the wrong thing, getting into another scrape. He finds it so difficult to conform. But then they are all individuals, not sheep. What a strange world, this, of teaching. So many roles played each day. In the morning I breakfast as myself; take on the role of confidant as I walk across the playground. In the staff room I become colleague, part of the school team; go to my form to be surrogate mother, sister, counsellor, peacemaker, and last but not least, teacher, imparter of knowledge and skills, encouraging the timid, trying to quieten the chatty and motivate all. In fact, try to be the impossible, all things to all people. No Jean Brodie me, but unchanging, yes, they rely on us not to change.

'How many weeks to half-term?' Asks one bright spark, exclaiming, 'Oh God!' When told seven.

'That's an age,' says another.

'Shut up,' shouts Ralph, 'So what if it is seven weeks, what do you care, you don't work anyway.'

The bell came to my rescue. A small child comes in with a note from the office. 'Not cover on the first day of term.' The brief note states that Mr Richards is off with a knee injury he got during pre-season rugby practise and I have to cover his next class. My heart sinks.

'Oh hell! Sorry God.'

Waiting at the door of the yet empty classroom, first year pupils drift in, timetable and map in hand.

'Is this RE Miss?'

'Where's Mr Richards, Miss?'

'What's your name Miss?'

'Are you taking us Miss?'

'Is this a Jesus lesson Miss?'

'Why do we have to do all this Jesus stuff Miss?'

I manage to cope only too glad to hand over to a colleague after my stint of cover. A last coffee before leaving. I have navigated the first day of term sanity intact. But what of tomorrow! I walk to my car through a now quiet playground, again humming the words,

'He married the girl with the strawberry curl, and the band played on.'

Island in the Sun

by

Kris White

'How ever did I get myself out here?' re-iterated Kim to herself for the ump-teenth time as she trudged her way up the dusty hill that boasted the main street of this proud little town. She was in the capital of a jewel of an island which had been exquisitely dropped into a tropical blue sea.

For the fourth time in as many hours she had made her way in the broiling heat between two Government offices - no escaping bureaucracy anywhere in this world - seeking the formal piece of paper that would allow her to stay here and work. This minute Third World country, barely the size of a pin head in the atlas, Kim hoped was to be her home for the next two years.

At last, with Work Permit clutched in clammy hands and as fast as yet another hill would allow - why do they always go up and never down, she pondered - she jauntily made her way towards the 250 bed hospital where her brief was to advise on and work with the up-dating of the administration. The sweat streaked face that reflected back at her as she glanced at a window when pushing open the sun battered wooden doors momentarily frightened her into wondering whether what should have been a heaven of blue skies and golden sunshine would, instead, turn out to be her downfall.

The sun's heat soon gave way to the basking warmth being extended by the man who was to be her boss. Thankfully sipping an ice cold juice in his office and with the luxuriously refreshing breeze from the fan lulling her into drowsiness, she was suddenly jolted back into reality when she heard Mr Ambrose say, '...but, of course, we want you to see what you are letting yourself in for before you decide whether to stay.' Instantly there flashed back into her mind the nagging words from her headquarters now so many miles away in London, '...it really is a bit of a mess out there ... you don't have to take on the assignment...'

Not without a little trepidation, Kim gamely followed him into the Medical Records Office to meet the two clerks running the section. As the elder of the two, a sparkling woman about thirty, stepped forward with outstretched hand the two of them knew instantly that a life-long friendship was just being born. By the same instinct the young English girl knew that never would there be any acceptance of her by the younger colleague. For the first time since arriving, Kim realized that simply because of the colour of her skin she had unwittingly been rejected out-of-hand. The sad hopelessness hit her as in the searing pain of early bereavement. And as the ease of mourning was best brought about by the passing of time, she hoped that time would also heal this ache.

She sensed the tension amongst the little group of hospital staff who by this time had gathered around, anxious to meet the newcomer and to see her reaction. As the adjacent door was opened - she knew why!

Never in her wildest dreams had she expected the sight that confronted her! A dark, musty room some twenty five feet long by perhaps sixteen feet wide; running round edges, tightly packed from floor to ceiling were files and, in the centre, undulating mountains of hundreds - no thousands - of unfiled case notes thrown higgeldy-piggeldy into piles. She was speechless! After the pause brought about by the shock, she slowly turned round to see steps of eyes peering round the door as the owners bent and stretched themselves round each other, eagerly awaiting her decision. In an instant those eyes told her all! Out of the window would have to go those seemingly wonderful plans made over the last few weeks. She knew that the next six months she was going to spend working flat out as a filing clerk. And that is exactly what she did.

From that moment began two of the happiest and most rewarding years of her life on an island that she came to look upon as her second home.

A welcoming party was thrown in the little office immediately that first day's work ended. Quite some welcoming party in fact, for Mr Ambrose saw to it that it continued every Friday after the chores were finished for months to come.

Indeed, celebrations seemed to be the order of the day in this little island so financially under privileged but so rich in warmth and hospitality. It was the all embracing web of welcome with its resulting sense of security that helped to allay Kim's fears of the hurricane season just about to start. The first night as she lay in the bare little room on the wooden slats that made for a bed, listening to the tropical rain lashing against the shutters whilst the thunder reverberated round the valley and the lightning turned night into day, she thrust her head beneath the sheet and thought,

'If they can live with it, so can I!' and ostensibly listening to 'The Last Night of the Proms' by courtesy of the overseas service of the BBC, was soon lost in a world of slumber.

Laboriously sifting and wading through nearly 90,000 files - although there were only 70,000 inhabitants on the island - she managed to reduce them to almost half by removing duplicated and triplicated information and with the aid of shelves provided by carpenters, the whole system was eventually revamped.

To corroborate much of the information, Kim needed to visit the tiny villages scattered throughout the densely wooded countryside. An official four-wheel drive vehicle with Chauffeur was assigned to her and many fantastic months were spent bumping unceremoniously along the dirt tracks, seriously known locally as roads, exploring the wonders of the stark sugar canefields and the banana plantations with the precious fruit swathed in its blue plastic to protect it from the elements ready for export. In their own special seasons grapefruits, mangoes, avocados, guavas - all waiting for passing hands to pick them - and all year round elegant breadfruit trees and palms swaying hundreds of feet above sea level with the breathtaking views scattered carelessly below. It was hard to accept the treachery of the magnificent white rollers of the Atlantic breaking over the golden sands; many others were also fooled for it was said that some half-a-dozen fishermen lost their battle with that ocean every year.

As time went on Kim realized more and more that priority had to be given to the Island and Hospital needs as they presented themselves rather than to her preconceived ideals, and steadfastly she worked to this end.

She marvelled at the way a colleague's three year old daughter would be dropped off at the hospital lunch times after morning school some four miles away by whoever happened to be walking or trucking that way about one o'clock. It never ceased to amaze Kim how a little one could be known to be in safe hands at any time without knowing whose hands they were.

Another cultural philosophy which impressed itself was the wailing of hordes who miraculously appeared at the hospital from all over the island when a patient died - so heartrending in their shrillness but within half-an-hour turned to joyous laughter and merrymaking.

For the first few weekends happy bands of islanders acted as guides and they would trek off laughing together through the underwood of the rain forests until the whole of the island had been criss-crossed. At the end of these exhausting expeditions Kim could never decide whether she was dripping wet from exertion, rain, the many frothy rivers waded through or a combination of all three. Whatever it was they were experiences she would treasure.

Ringing in her ears too would be the laughter and the music from the steel bands whilst dancing on the beaches and swimming in the tepid sea at midnight under the glow of the full moon and the luscious barbecued chicken which followed. It seemed to her that chicken would never taste the same again anywhere.

All too soon the end of the sojourn loomed into sight and with it the inevitable round of farewell parties that only these people knew how to put on to perfection. Kim's delight at this feting was marred by the fear of not knowing how to take her leave from this isle of paradise without making a fool of herself.

She had no need to worry though, for so well was she ingratiated into her second home that the unspoken thoughts were acknowledged and respected by all and it was only her physical being that was alone as she made her journey to the little airstrip. And as the tiny twelve seater 'plane lifted into the air she knew without doubt that she would be back.

A Question Not Worth Asking

by

Sandy Johns

She'd always had a dread feeling for the post that arrived on a Monday morning, more so than any other day of the week. It seemed that everything was thrown into sharp relief on a Monday - a day for extra late oversleeping, extra wet rain; altogether an impressively terrible day for running out of toilet roll. And now the thump of an anonymous brown envelope on the doormat. The coconut matting scraped her bitten fingernails as she picked up the letter and examined the stamp, the postmark, the front, the back for clues. It always helped soften the blow to have a minute's preparation - a 'Seeboard' frank mark or a 'Please return to ...' on the flap - but this one was giving nothing away. True, the writing looked vaguely familiar; she toyed with the idea of opening it while she wrestled with the warped front door. Glancing left and right, she paused only to curse the milkman who had forgotten the semi-skimmed again, and returned to her squalid kitchen.

Looking round the rented flat, own entrance, sep. kit., ch., hc, month in advance, she resisted the temptation to wonder how she had come to this. True, Mum was right, the typing was something to fall back on, and yes, she did have a secure-enough job for these days, and her superannuation was maturing as she did, but nothing had really moved on in her life at all. Or was standing still going backwards?

In the depths of her dressing gown pocket, amongst the cigarettes, lighter, sellotape, hardened scrunch of tissue - the Bessie Glass survival kit for life's challenges - she rediscovered the dog-eared envelope over her cup of milkless coffee. She sat at the table to read. What should have been her contemplation space, her scrubbed pine table in a sun-streamed bay window, fluffy cat on window-sill amongst the winter jasmine. The cracked formica did little to enhance her concession to Habitat, the terracotta herb pot even now bristling with dead and dying herbs; this in turn did little to enhance the Kentucky fried chicken she usually grabbed on the way home for dinner. The overview of leafy, glady Holland Park squares, or in this case the electricity substation that separated her yard and Hezbollah House was best ignored. She dived into the letter.

She knew now why the handwriting looked familiar; it was convent-girl scrawl, what all those years of learning italic handwriting turned into, like the South-London-cool accents that were the results of Miss Pocock's elocution lessons. Marked for life by their strange angular letters and their proper grammar, improper for today, which kept rearing its outmoded head, these convent girls were out there somewhere, scattered to the four winds for life. Except that they weren't, they were here knocking on her door or rather landing on her mat.

'Dear Tessa, I'm sure you won't remember me ...' Cathy Standish? Well, you're right there, unless you were the one with plastic kneecaps - but wasn't her name ... oh, never mind. '...reunion next year ...list of names.' My God, she's serious thought Tessa, leafing through the instructions of colour coding for those contacted, those replied and, presumably, those in a nice safe ward somewhere, cuddling their teddies. Names from a distant past - more distant than she would have cared to admit, twenty years for Christ's sake - leapt up and nutted her. 'Gels' who were now BBC journalists appeared before her with pigtails and scabby knees. My God, she couldn't be in the Army. Why am I surprised, what on earth else could she ever have been? Oh and Isa, beautiful Isa, what about her ...'

Tess gave up on the idea of going to work at that point. Sod them, would the Crown Estate Commissioners really miss her? She doubted it. The temps bashed out the letters and she checked them for illiteracy. She had to play this one carefully - the (male) ego of the Estates Officers couldn't take too much correction. This was her only real responsibility and her reward was to be allowed to walk up the hallowed halls of Carlton House Terrace - the senior ranks were allowed carpet on the floors! - to get them signed. 'I dare say they'll be running round like headless chickens when they realise they'll actually have to come downstairs and talk to the temps personally,' she thought to herself as she snuggled down with her coffee into the lumpy armchair.

Her head swam with images of twenty years ago and imaginings of the present. Names she couldn't place, faces she couldn't name. How would she appear to them. Her mind wandered down a rather fruitless path of how she would present herself - long earrings and bright clothes, Anita Roddick of the Civil Service? Or refined and ladylike, black bow at nape, pearls subtly nestling, very Dorking. No, they's never believe than. She smiled wryly to herself and then caught sight of herself reflected in the window, a blotchy pink woman in a dressing gown resting before Hezbollah House, and she gave up. The truth was that she was grey; she'd been nowhere, she'd done nothing. No travel. No lovers. Nothing ventured. Nothing gained. She'd fallen back on her typing be-

137

fore she'd even tried falling off anything else. She pondered the depressing truth as her coffee got cold and the schoolgirl scrawl on the blue notepaper drifted to the floor. It wasn't that she was fat, it wasn't a Woman's Own job, a question of blonde highlights and where to put your blusher. A trip to South Moulton Street wouldn't get to grips with the problem. She saw no solution in a wild moment of window smashing, clothes ripping, screaming, screaming, and then to a quiet garden somewhere. She saw no solution in back to the train, back to the LVs, back to the wall. The inevitable gripped her hand as she reached out and sobbed, without regret, at the chocolate munching reflection in the glass. It was all a question of knowing what questions not to ask.

Living Doll

by

Mary Green

Carole was early. At the far end of the hall she could see the barman checking his stock and over in the corner, reading his evening paper, sat the regular DJ for Sam's Sensational Sixties Nite. Neither looked up as Carole walked through the swing doors. She hesitated, unsure whether to stay or go. The emptiness made her feel exposed and she looked around for a hiding place.

The tap of her high heels echoed loudly as she walked across the wooden floor towards the Ladies Cloakroom. She pushed open the door, blinking at the brightness of the fluorescent lights. They were stark and unforgiving on her carefully applied make up. Despondently she stared back at her reflection.

'Shall I have one more go, or shall I leave it,' she murmured to herself. Reaching for her bag, she glanced down as she did so and saw that her hands were shaking.

She sighed. 'Well, that's that, you'll just have to do. Lucky for you that you're not on the hunt for Mr Right,' she told herself.

Carole took a step back, shook her head of freshly shampooed hair and pouted at her reflection.

'Will he recognise me after all this time,' she wondered. It was all so long ago. She had been a child.

She turned sideways, looking back at herself over her shoulder. 'Suppose he doesn't realise who I am when I walk up and say ....'

Her body froze. Her mind became a fog. Say what? Suddenly she felt sick with nerves and put her hands on the side of the wash basin to steady herself. The door to the cloakroom was pushed open and two other girls came in, eager and excited at the prospect of a night out. They were giggling and nudging one another but when they saw Carole semi-slumped over the basin they hesitated.

'Are you OK?' one asked, taking a step towards her.

'Oh yes, fine thanks.' Carole lifted her head. There were beads of sweat above her upper lip yet she felt cold and gave a small shiver. 'Just been rushing a bit. Forgot to have lunch.'

When the two girls had gone Carole shuffled her way down the cloakroom to the attendant's room. It was empty and closing the door behind her she slowly

139

sat down. The black chair seat was hard and felt cold through her thin dress. She shivered again whilst looking around for inspiration and courage. A telephone number was scrawled across one wall and a 'Tracy woz 'ere', but nothing to help her with an opening line to bridge the years of separation.

She sighed and closed her eyes. For so long she had waited for a chance like this, now it had arrived and she felt at a loss. 'Maybe I can make a record request,' she thought, 'and then I'll walk across the floor towards him as Cliff sings 'Got myself a crying, talking, sleeping, walking, Livin' Doll'. Then there will be no need for words, the years will fall away, he'll lift me up high and whirl me round making me shriek with delight.'

Without warning the years rolled back and Carole was a child again. Loving, trusting, a real living doll. She felt his strong arms around her, heard his deep rolling laugh ringing in her ears. The moment passed and she opened her eyes abruptly. They began to fill with tears.

'You stupid cow!' She muttered angrily. 'Who the hell are you kidding. Lift you up high. Not without risk of a hernia he won't.' She shifted in the chair, straightening herself and pulling in her stomach. His Living Doll had grown and gained weight since the days when their home throbbed to the beat of The Dave Clark Five, Gerry and The Pacemakers, The Beatles, The Stones and, of course, Cliff.

Carole brushed at the tears with the back of her hand and sniffed. 'Oh how he'd loved his Sixties music. So had Mum, despite her complaints that he'd got stuck in the groove and that it was time he grew up and started behaving like a responsible husband and father.' She sighed. 'Poor Mum, she was asking for the impossible.'

'Why can I never isolate the good times?' She thought, as the tears flowed. 'Why must the shouting and the sound of breaking glass follow through relentlessly.' And the past flooded her mind. The nights she'd lain in bed listening as he tried to find his way through the front door; the mornings she'd found him fully dressed, asleep on the floor where he'd fallen, cloaked in the choking smell of staleness. She remembered too her confusion of feelings. Loving him, yet hating him for the pain he caused.

The images were sharp and fresh and as Carole rummaged in her handbag for a tissue her thoughts rushed cruelly on. On to the night when he wrenched an iron stake from the fence and battered his way into their home in a fit of alcoholic frustration. The terrible noise had drawn Carole out of bed and as she'd reached the top of the stairs the front door caved in and he'd staggered forward, wielding the iron bar. The wild and terrifying sight stayed in her nightmares long after he had left.

The day he went away he held her tight, kissed her and made a great many promises. She believed them all. They would keep in touch, he'd come and see her regularly, take her on holidays and would always love his Living Doll.

'Why did you never call me?' she whispered. 'I loved you so, I needed you.'

Carole blew her nose hard and realised that she felt cold and stiff. How long had she been sitting in the strange little room on a hard chair? Gingerly she pushed herself up and her knees cracked as she rose slowly to her feet, thankful that she had not been disturbed, but anxious once more about her appearance.

'I must look a real mess,' she sighed as she slipped out of her small refuge and into the main cloakroom area.

Music drifted through from the hall telling her that the Sensational Sixties Nite had begun. The face reflected in the mirror was streaked with black waterproof mascara but Carole could feel the soul behind the puffy eyes begin to lift. It had heard the beat of the drums and bass guitar and knew that the ache of waiting would soon be over.

Carole splashed her face with cold water and did a repair job on her face before pushing open the door and stepping back into the hall which was now pulsating with life. The hot, smokey air stung her raw eyes as she made her way towards the far end of the hall, sure of finding him there. But vainly she pushed her way around the bar, reacting twice to false hopes.

Slowly she walked back to the main door and sat down by the wall opposite. An hour passed as she waited, watching the swing doors as people came and went and she heard her Mum's voice sound loudly in her head. 'It's not that I don't think you should see him, it's just that I don't want you hurt again. He's so unreliable. Always promising the world.'

'Poor disappointed Mum,' thought Carole, a wave of sympathy washing over her. She'd seen him at last month's Sixties Nite and it had really unsettled her. She would not be coming here again.

'Did he ask after me?' Carole had queried.

'I saw him. I did not speak to him.' Her Mum had sniffed.

'So here I am,' thought Carole, 'still waiting for the man who is always in my heart. We are a part of each other and he is the best I can ever have.'

She was hardly aware of the music as she sat, her eyes fixed on the doors, patiently waiting. Suddenly he was there, swaying slightly and blinking into the bright lights. Carole gripped the edge of her chair and stared open mouthed at the man who had pushed through the doors. Aware of the change in herself, he

141

had remained unaltered in her imagination. She looked at her once broad shouldered, sturdy hero and saw he was slightly balding. She also noted, as he hitched at his trousers in an attempt to tuck it away, that he had gained a beer gut. Yet there was no doubt in her mind, this was her man.

As he turned and moved towards the bar Carole jumped to her feet instinctively reaching out for the sleeve of his jacket. Her fingers clutched at it and gave two small tugs before dropping her hand into his.

The middle aged man turned and blinked at the tense young woman who had suddenly appeared beside him.

Carole held her breath and for a moment her courage faltered. But then her smile emerged and grew wider as recognition slowly crept into the man's pink, watery eyes.

'Good God!' he exclaimed.

'Hello Dad,' Carole replied.

Y Hendref

by

Glyn Randell

He turned off left from the 'A' road as on the map. It had to be correct. There was the public car park on his left. So far so good! The road wound on ahead, writhing and bending in the characteristic fashion of Welsh roads.

'The rolling English drunkard made the rolling English road,' he mused, 'Except that was England.'

The Welsh bends were daunting, each to be taken quite seriously. Life would have been easier if he had been driving a car. The small removal van was not so manoeuvrable. Care was vital for everything, or perhaps most of what he had was in the back.

A new life was beginning. After two redundancies, the need to leave the rat-race was imperative. Thank God, he was alone! He had put all his money together, and here he was on his way to his new home. What was it the estate agent had said, 'A Welsh Farm House slightly remote from the village.' He had fallen in love with it immediately. Sure it was rather run down, and about a ten minute walk from the village, but it had character plus a lovely big garden.

Thank goodness the weather was fine. On the left, true to the map a large lake appeared. He could see a few sailing boats. A mile or so further was the forest, and then the turning to the right. Look out for the next turning on the right about a half mile further on and ...yes here it was! He swung the wheel over and started to brave the narrow lane. It would uphill for about fifty yards then turn sharp left. As he was turning into the bend, he noticed a neglected chapel on the right lying a little back from the road.

Then there was a blinding flash followed by a tremendous clap of thunder. It was as though a giant hand seized the van by its bonnet and held it motionless. The windscreen illuminated like a video screen. A woman's face appeared, but oh what a face! On her head was a black stove pipe hat. Strands of hair, green, blue, and red peeped from it and fell around the face. Her nose was long and pointed, her cheeks sunken, and her mouth full of yellow twisted tombstones masquerading as teeth. But her eyes!... they were green and luminous. They bored hypnotically into his.

'Welcome,' she shrilled, 'Welcome, I have waited for you so long.'

Then he was turning the bend. All was normal. He shook himself, 'I've been driving too long,' he told himself, 'I've dozed off. It was a dream!'

About fifty yards further on was the house. It was typically double fronted with slate roof, sash windows and front door within an open porch. It stood on the left of the road, proud yet sombre in its garment of sand brick. It looked, a place which had survived many generations of humans. He pulled up, then just sat. His reverie was interrupted by a voice.

'Mr Hammond?'

He returned to reality.

'Oh yes!'

The owner of the voice was a stocky little man with dark curly hair, brown eyes and a weather beaten face.

'Davies. Come to help you like you asked. My mate's in the house. He's Jones, Tom Jones, only he doesn't sing like...' They both laughed.

It took perhaps a couple of hours but between the three of them finally the van was unloaded and his few things were installed in the farmhouse. Hammond paid both the men. He declined an invitation to the pub.

Having made up his bed, drunk several mugs of tea, and fixed himself supper, he settled down to watch the 'box'. It had been a long day, and he began to doze. Bed was calling and he heard it. As he went off to sleep he could hear a rustling in the loft above. He thought, 'Mice! I'll have to get a cat.'

When he awakened the next morning there was something tickling his face. He brushed his hand across and removed a spider's web. 'Cobweb,' he thought, 'Must have a spring clean.'

After breakfast he loaded the motor scooter he had brought with him into the van. The removal van had been hired and he had arranged to return it to agents in a nearby town. As he drove again down the lane past the chapel a slight shiver went through him as he recollected his odd dream. The ride back was good. He took the mountain road, bumped over the cattle grids, talked to the sheep, admired the views, and luxuriated in the drama of the mountain scenery.

There was a path across the fields to the village, and the following day he used it. He needed supplies and was reluctant to pass the old chapel, and relieved not to have to do so.

The village shop looked after as many of the needs of the inhabitants as possible. It was Post Office, grocer, greengrocer, and even sold paraffin oil. He went in, and bought what he needed.

'Are you up at the Parry's old place,' asked the lady as she took his money.

'Yes,' he said.

'Getting on ok?'

'Fine. Thanks. Well goodbye.'

'Bye Dear.'

His days passed busily. There was much to do. The house needed a great deal of work to make it habitable. He wondered about the previous occupants. What sort of people were they? There were so many spiders webs. He seemed forever to be brushing them from his face, but it was the countryside and that perhaps explained it.

He went down to the shop frequently and drank pints in the pub. People were very kind and genuinely interested in the newcomer.

'We have a grand choir here. They've even been to America to sing. You must come down to rehearsal on Thursday evening to hear them. Do you sing?'

'Sorry no.'

'Pity.'

During one of his strolls around the village he met Mrs Thomas. She made no secret that she was delighted to make his acquaintance as she wanted to practice her English. Most village folk preferred to speak Welsh so his presence was most welcome! She was quite willing to talk about the Parry's.

She told him, 'The Parry's had lived in that 'hendref' for generations.'

'Hendref?'

'It's Welsh for Winter farmhouse. In the old days the Welsh farmers brought their animals down from the mountains and spent the winter in the 'hendref.' There aren't many of these farmhouses left except the ones someone has cared for.'

'I see.'

'They were lovely people and they were having trouble. Money!'

'Was that why they left?'

'Bless you no! No we don't know why they left. They went and left everything as it was,' she smiled, 'just like Marie Celeste.'

'What happened then?'

'It got sorted out but nobody ever saw the Parry's again. They just vanished!'

'Did anyone else come in?'

'Oh yes quite one or two but they all went off and they never seemed to say goodbye to anyone.'

'How curious!'

He went back home feeling puzzled and apprehensive. The rustling was becoming more audible. He had borrowed a cat and tried to introduce it into the loft but it ran away from the house.

Evening was setting in. He took a book from the bookcase and tried to read. The noise was becoming louder, concentration was difficult, and an aura of evil surrounded the house.

Night came, but sleep was impossible. He sat watching the door. There was a knock and he was drawn towards it. Mesmerised, he opened it. She stood outside, the same face he had seen in his dream.

'I have come for you,' she whispered.

He backed into the room until he met the bookcase.

Gradually she turned into a huge spider. It cast its web towards him and he felt the fibres reaching his body. Fighting against them his hand reached and grasped a book. He threw it. There was a flash and a terrible scream as the thing erupted into incandescent light, burned, fizzled and was gone leaving only a small wet patch on the floor. The book was lying on top of it. Considerably shaken he staggered forward to pick it up. A copy of the Bible was in his hand. The room was suddenly full of people.

'The trouble with this case,' said the presiding judiciary expert at the hearing which ensued, 'is that there is nothing remaining on the statute book to deal with witches or compensation for their victims. Nevertheless ladies and gentlemen shall we proceed!'

Taken for a Ride

by

E R Healey

Ken closed the front door carefully behind him and set off for work, still feeling dejected. It wasn't just going back to Malton Bus Depot after a few days off, but also the certainty that his wife was still hurt by his outburst the previous evening. Why couldn't he control his temper, he asked himself, suddenly crashing the car gears. The price of the clock repair wasn't that high really, and certainly didn't justify the way he'd yelled at Sylvia over supper.

The three days had been going so well: shopping together, a meal out, and time to catch up on odd jobs round the house. Which reminds me, thought Ken, I've got those metal corners for Derek's workbench in my cash pouch. I wonder what route he's on this week and more to the point, which I'm on? I suppose I'll have to see that bully Bates first thing. What a welcome back to the depot!

'You can't park there! Where've you been all week?' demanded the car park attendant. 'Remember Management's new plan? Bus drivers' cars down at Riverside, mate.' Ken felt the familiar surge of irritation but managed to hold it in. Not having allowed for a walk back from Riverside, he knew that time was now against him.

Ten minutes later, his bag and cap bumping against his leg, Ken lurched through the depot, dodging diesel spills.

'Ken! Ken! You're back!' The young lad in his still smart uniform jumped off a bus platform as he passed.

'Derek - look, I'll see you later. I'm late now and Bates will be in one of his moods...'

Bates was. 'You're late again, Hughes!' he thundered. 'Can't you ever be on time? I'm trying to run a schedule here! How can I get buses running smoothly when my drivers don't bother to turn up on time, eh?'

Ken swallowed, clenched his fists and felt himself flushing. Telling himself that Bates was right, that he was only doing his job, he opened his mouth, trying to force himself to apologize.

'I don't want to hear any more of your excuses, Hughes. Get out of here and get your bus out - now!'

147

Bates' little eyes were almost invisible in his distorted red face. Ken's own fury swamped his self-control and he heard himself yell, 'If the management of this place changes parking regulations without warning workers what d'you expect? I've been off three days, remember. How was I to know - telepathy?'

Bates glared at him, breathing heavily. Then he spoke, slowly and menacingly.

'I said no excuses, Hughes. If you can't cope with this job you'd better pick your money up at the end of the week. And good riddance!'

Ken stared blankly, realizing he'd gone too far. This damned temper of his! He thought of Sylvia, of their Spanish holiday planned for September. It took a tremendous effort to mutter 'No need for that, Mr Bates. I'm here to work. What route am I on?'

Bates' face twitched, sensing triumph. 'Fourteen. The Pension Run. Knew you'd enjoy that, Hughes. Now get out of my office!'

Resisting the urge to slam the door, Ken set off for the despised Pension Bus. Actually, he quite enjoyed its slow pace and the inevitable chats with all the elderly passengers, excited about their weekly trip into Malton, but he would never have admitted it. Today it would be quite soothing! He swung himself aboard, unlocked the cash-box and took a few deep breaths. I must calm down, he thought. His heart was still thumping, partly from righteous indignation and partly from the shock of staring unemployment in the face. He had nearly lost everything because of that row with Bates.

Some time later, his mood much lighter, Ken was manoeuvring his bus along country lanes to the next stop. Most of the regulars were aboard already: Mrs Fox and Miss Pringle catching up on the week's gossip, Mrs Ambarrow and her spaniel Amy, Colonel and Mrs Dillon, and the usual six or seven from Sleep Hollow Residential Home. He didn't know the others so well although most of them had greeted him as they clambered up the steps. Occasionally somebody younger than sixty used the bus - today a young man had got on at Little Ham - but normally by the time he'd collected everyone there would be forty or more smartly-dressed pensioners aboard. Thursday was the Red Cross Centre's day in Malton, he knew that.

'And not only that, driver,' Miss Emmerson had told him as she collected her ticket, 'the Shopping Precinct Cafe has special Senior Citizens' rates on a Thursday now. Isn't that nice?'

'You go and have a cup of tea there for me, Miss Emmerson,' he told her with a grin. 'You'll need it if you fill all that trolley with shopping.'

After three more villages, the bus had a clear run on country lanes before the outskirts of Malton. Having emptied the cash-box into the pouch at his feet, Ken pushed back his cap and settled down to enjoy this stretch. He was only half-aware of his passengers chattering or dozing behind him. Suddenly a movement in the mirror caught his eye. He slowed down slightly as the young man from Little Ham, hunched in a grubby parka, picked his way right down the bus. To Ken's astonishment, he held a piece of paper over the steering-wheel grunting, 'Don't want to start a panic among the grannies, do we, mate?'

As he let the speed die down, Ken read 'Hand over the money. And let me off. I have a gun.' Glancing sideways, Ken saw a threatening shape in the man's pocket and a second look, at his face, revealed tension and grim determination. The hand in the pocket gestured and Ken started to apply the brakes, thinking quickly.

Suddenly the enormity of it struck him. This young idiot was threatening *him*, was going to steal *his* takings. Indignation swept over him and he had a struggle to keep his hands from shaking. At the same time, an inner voice warned him to keep his temper and he relived the shock he'd felt in his supervisor's office that morning. Carefully, he eased the bus into a layby and reached down for the leather pouch. He visualized himself swinging it heavily into the man's stomach, disabling him, but he knew that was a television move that wouldn't work.

'The cash too!' growled the man. Ken flicked the key on the cash-box to reveal only a couple of coins.

'It's all in there, you fool' he said. 'Now get off my bus.'

Clutching the bulky pouch, the stranger swung off the platform and looked around at the empty fields as Ken quickly pulled out into the traffic-free road.

'Funny place to get off,' commented Colonel Dillon, twisting round on the front seat. 'Just standing there, d'you see? What's he doing now? Emptying something on the ground?'

'Nothing to worry about, Colonel,' said Ken jubilantly. 'It's just two chunks of metal and lots of little bits of useless plastic, like your bus tokens!'

149

Final Proof

by

Peter Batchelor

'How much do you love me?' she would ask, always with that certain look.

'Too much,' he'd say solemnly.

'Prove it!'

It was their private joke; a special little game they had played on and off for over forty years, ever since that first time at the carnival on the village green.

Now, as he climbed the stairs of the cottage, clutching his carefully prepared tray with its bowl of clear soup, the wafer-thin slice of bread and the small dish of ice-cream, all set on a delicate lace cloth, Robert remembered with a sudden, agonising clarity. For a moment, he could see the Ferris wheel spinning like some gigantic firework against the night sky; smell the heady aroma of candy-floss and diesel; hear the churning music of the hurdy-gurdy and the raucous shouts of the stall holders...

In a light summer dress, with her long, streaming auburn hair and her eyes bright with happiness, Rachel had never looked more beautiful. They had strolled, hand in hand, across the straw-covered grass into that whirling kaleidoscope of colour and sound, each joyously aware that the magic was as much in themselves as in their surroundings.

'How much do you love me?' she had asked, giving him that wicked smile.

He had said the first thing that came into his head because he knew already that no words could truly express what he felt.

'Too much,' he told her.

Laughing, she clapped her hands with delight. 'Prove it!'

'How?' he demanded, and when she shrugged he had grabbed a ball from a nearby coconut-shy and hurled it with all the exuberance of a young man on the threshold of a glorious adventure.

Miraculously, he had knocked down no less than three coconuts as the ball ricochetted from one to another, and he won a huge, garishly-painted doll with corkscrew curls and a decided squint.

They had collapsed with laughter before Rachel went suddenly quiet, reaching up to touch his face and saying it was the nicest present anyone had ever given her and that she'd treasure it as long as she lived.

150

The second time she had issued her mischievous challenge, they were enjoy-ing a woodland picnic, close to a fast-moving stream. Robert had immediately jumped up and crossed to the opposite bank by balancing precariously on a line of slippery stones.

'My hero!' Rachel had cried, and just as he was making a triumphant, arm-waving return, he had toppled backwards into the water, emerging moments later covered in wet green weed and vowing darkly, between their paroxysms of mirth, never again to be lured into attempting to prove his devotion.

After that, of course, Rachel had delighted in doing it time after time, when-ever the mood took her. They might be sitting on a park bench or looking in a shop window; riding on a bus or dancing in the village hall. Whenever and wherever, Robert always tried to be equal to the occasion. Sometimes it was difficult; sometimes not difficult at all.

On their wedding night, Rachel had stood proudly before him in the bedroom of the sea-side guest-house where they spent their honeymoon. In the glow from the bedside lamp, her long auburn hair was like a flame around her nakedness.

'How much do you love me?' she had asked softly, never taking her eyes off his. He had tried to keep his answer light-hearted, but his voice sounded strangely hoarse.

'Prove it,' she whispered, and he had found it very easy indeed.

It was a different story the day Rachel lost the baby for which they had tried so long. From her hospital bed, eyes brimming with tears, she had forced a brave smile and attempted to go through the familiar routine as Robert sat numbly by her side. For once, her tremulous request for proof had left him at a complete loss. All he could do was hold her in his arms while she wept as though her heart would break. Later, he had gone out and pawned his most precious possession; a solid gold pocket-watch left to him by his father. He had had some half-formed notion of using the money to take Rachel on a long holi-day to help ease her pain and, hopefully, hasten the healing process. When she discovered what he had done, she was horrified and refused to rest until the watch had been redeemed.

'That was all because of my silly game,' she had remonstrated, both with her-self and him. 'Surely you know you don't really have to prove anything?'

Nevertheless, as their lives proceeded, unremarkably for the most part, she continued to issue her little challenges on various occasions, and Robert always strove not to disappoint her. It was part of the magic of their relationship.

Thirty years on, that magic was still there and, indeed, Rachel, true to form, had produced the time-honoured question as they celebrated Robert's sixty-fifth birthday.

'How much do you love me?' she'd demanded, smiling fondly at him across the top of her glass of champagne.

'Too much,' Robert dutifully replied.

'Prove it!'

With a flourish he had produced his brand-new bus pass, collected by him that very morning from the village post office.

'Ride with me into the sunset!' he'd cried, and when the laughter had subsided and she kissed him, it was just as though all the years since that night at the carnival had simply melted away...

A sudden sound, halfway between a sigh and a moan, brought Robert abruptly back to the present as he reached the top of the stairs. Balancing the tray with one hand, he opened the bedroom door, hoping desperately that the tiny, shrunken figure lying on the bed wouldn't see the terrible sadness that he knew must be in his eyes.

'Thought I might be able to tempt you,' he said cheerfully, nodding towards the contents of the tray.

Rachel moved her head a fraction and tried to smile. Her hair, greying now but still luxuriant, fanned out on the pillow, making her pale face look even smaller.

'Not really hungry,' she whispered.

Robert crooked his arm beneath her thin shoulders. 'Just a few mouthfuls - for me,' he urged her.

She opened her mouth and promptly retched as the first spoonful of warm liquid touched her lips. Struggling to try again, she suddenly stiffened, moaning softly as more pain knifed through her wasted body. Her eyes swivelled towards the small brown bottle lying on her bedside table.

'Time ... for ... my ... pill,' she gasped

Robert felt a wave of black despair. He knew the bottle was empty; that she had already had today's dosage; that the nurse wouldn't be calling again until tomorrow... Why, in God's name, hadn't they kept her in hospital? The bitterness welled up inside him as he recalled the doctor's voice blandly telling him things he had tried desperately not to hear: '... shortage of beds ... might as well be at home... two months, maybe three at the most ... terribly sorry, old chap ...'

Miserably, he put down the tray and smoothed Rachel's damp brow.

'Nurse will be here first thing in the morning, love ...' he began desperately.

She swallowed and tried to smile through her pain. 'How much do you love me?' she asked weakly.

He choked on his reply. 'Too much.'

'Prove it,' she murmured, closing her eyes.

With tears streaming down his stubbled cheeks, Robert kissed her for the last time. Then he picked up the spare pillow.

Lisa

by

Malcolm Ashton

It was there. Again. In the sky. The light in the sky, the sweet iridescent purity of a light that glowed for her, for her dead child, for all the sweetness and love that she would never have. The light in the sky was there.

Quickly she combed her thick black hair, touching and bobbing the soft ringlets with her fingers as she did. She wanted to look nice for Maria. It was quite a long walk, almost two miles, so she hurriedly changed into a pair of flat shoes and her fingers were trembling and numb with excitement. She pulled a headscarf round her head in case it rained, buttoned her coat and picked up her handbag. It took her almost an hour to walk the distance. She was overweight and quite unfit. The last half mile was up a long straight road that led directly to the downs and she heaved and puffed her way up the slope, tired, sweating with the effort even in the harsh cold that had crushed the grass slopes into a tumbled mass of white feathered slur. She stopped and looked around. The moon seemed to peek at her. She was all alone. At the top of the hill she stopped for a moment and looked about her. The low slopes of grass, covered in frost were laid out like giant white wastelands, the houses and tower blocks of the town below appeared magical and mystical in the keen white light from the moon, everywhere there was a bitter tang of cold and whiteness, in the air, in the sky, in the bushes and the grass. Everywhere there was cold. Except in her heart.

Where was the light? Where was it! She stood for a moment, puffing, still with the effort of the hill in her bones, she stood with tears in her eyes and her heart overflowing with love. Each touch, each tang of the chill night air against her unprotected legs and hands and face overcame her with a deepness and a feeling she could not describe. Maria. How she yearned, how she cried for Maria, her sweet child, her baby, her little girl with her black baby ringlets and huge eyes, her face a picture, her tiny chubby hands and puckered fingers, soft and plucked with dimples and biscuit crumbs. How the love opened in her heart, how the tears dropped, crushed in her eyes like drops of grief, each tear a trove of love, each sob a simpleness. Her breasts heaved. The peace was like a cure. She sobbed, openly in the night air, unheeding of the cold that attacked

154

her open skin and flailed round her face like a viper, she wept and wept in the white light, basking and drowning in her own misery and love. How she yearned for her child.

A long while passed, a long while, and gradually the tears were squeezed dry, she stopped panting and she became calmer. How long had she been here?

She looked up at the moon and her chin wobbled in the cold. There was no light from the Other Side. Only the sterile moonlight sparkling in her eyes. She shivered and a long shudder hung through her body and touched her spine and shoulders. No sign of Maria. No sign at all.

She waited, still bursting with love, her heart an open wound, her eyes starry, straining into the sky and darkness, unwilling, unable to move away. For two nights in a row the light had appeared and she had been careful to stay indoors. This was the third night, the night Madame had said that she would see Maria. But there was nothing. Just darkness and ice. She waited, shivering, her toes and fingers numb, her face a cold white mask. Secretly, secretly, slowly, carefully, easily, slowly. The light was beginning to change.

Now the shivers ran up her spine like magic, like electric shocks. She gasped, looked away, breathed in and looked again. The light was stronger, eerily coloured, a pale orange, luminescent, sealing off the light from the moon, casting a weird orange glow over the soft silken snow, brightening the ground, becoming bolder, deeper, much deeper, orange, deep orange, flaming, flinging orange secrets to the frost-covered grass, merging into the air and the atmosphere like a magical mist.

She breathed in. She waited. She was surrounded with the breath from her child, nascent, her own blood and flesh tinged with fission.

Now the deep burr of orange grew deeper, deeper, it gave way to the first flush of crimson blossom that set a flush to her open face, caved inwards and blew apart, like blood from a mist, like the blood-red frost, the deep red opened in the sky, a hugeness of red that set a shape shimmering in the sky, streaks of glowing red carved in the face of a child. The child's mouth opened, the eyes closed, the soft, black ringlets fell about the face, the vaunted cry came out through the red mist.

'*Mama!*'

A mighty scream swept from the depths of her breast, a gargantuan agonised scream, full of hope and misery, like a drowning man hanging on a thread, she cried and screamed like a bitch, she swept her head back and cried into the air and the red mist, and all awhile the sky cast the billowing face into yet more agonising tantalising features and expressions she had once seen in her baby's face.

She did not know how long she stood there. She never knew. But eventually the sopping beautiful face began to fade, the crimson mist turned orange, she felt again the cold clasp of freezing mist clammy and stiff against her open skin, the orange faded to deep yellow, then saffron, the yellow became paler, the mist took over the hollows of the sky and she was alone again. She stood for a long long while, unable to let go, unable to turn and trudge homewards, waiting for a sign, a notion, straining her eyes and ears for an age, she stood like a statue and moved barely a muscle for hour after hour after hour. Time spun in her head but it meant nothing.

It was dawn when she eventually turned and walked slowly back down the long straight road. The first sparklets of sun cut through the mist and as she turned to look back at the empty sky, the depth of the new light cut into her soul, blinding her. She trudged ever onwards, still casting another look back every few seconds, hungering for a sign that would not come. It was only as she reached the end of the downs road and the flat frost-whitened grass gave way to thick hedge and tarmac that she suddenly realised how desperately cold and tired she was. She walked very slowly, her mind tumbling with the sights she had seen, the feelings she had felt.

The distance seemed to pass like magic, she never remembered walking home, but then she was walking towards her own front door, past the evergreens and the resident red squirrel out for a late autumnal glean. She reached in her bag for the key. Inside she kicked off her shoes and switched on the oven to heat the kitchen. She made a pot of tea, poured a cup, used plenty of milk and sugar and sat by the cold gas fire in her lounge sipping hot tea for a full five minutes before she realised the fire was not on. She finished the tea and looked at her watch. It was eight-fifty. Quickly she reached for the phone and rang the shop. Mr Lumas, the manager, answered the phone. Her voice was jerky.

'Hello - Mr Lumas - yes, it's me, Lisa - so sorry - I no come in today - I sick - very sick - go see doctor - yes - very sorry - very very sorry.'

She replaced the phone. Her hands were shaking and her heart was beating very fast. She lit the gas fire and went to make another pot of tea while the room warmed up. The kitchen was small and it had warmed up quickly with the heat from the oven. She sank down near the hot oven, thankful to be in the warmth, listening to the rising tone from the kettle and a tear touched her eye.

It was Maria. It had been Maria. She knew above all else, with a mother's heart that she had seen her child, seen her face, watched her, listened to her cry out in the haunted stillness of a black November night. The kettle boiled. The tea was made. Wistfully she gazed into the distance, through the window, thought of her child and her dire haunted cries.

A Glimmer in the Gutter

by

James Morrison

If I can reach the end of this road maybe I can escape. Must be residential buildings, but so high and inaccessible. Damn tower blocks. Damn architects. Maybe I can make some noise, smash a car. Why aren't there any lights on? Half past two in the morning is the answer I suppose. So cold and quiet. Must run. He's gaining. Faster. Quicker. Listen to his breath. If he catches me, he'll demand the money and beat me to a pulp. Shit, I'm scared. Come on legs. Why's it so quiet? Where's a car? He's shouting now. So eerie. Damp and misty. Sounds like he's all over the place. Damn, I'm running away from people. This looks like a park. Ah, there's a road. Only businesses though. Shit. A dead end. Fuck. Oh God.

'Gotchya now ya bastard.' Why does it echo so much? Look at him. A picture of respectability. Oh shit. The photos! Will he find them?

'Alright you bastard... ' He's stopping for breath. He's more knackered than me. There's a chance yet. Look at him. I can't believe it. Trenchcoat, suit.

'... Gimme the money.' Shall I? Look at this place. Dark, dank. No lights. Well, one or two. Misty. Smells odd too. Musty. One car. Where the hell am I? You start off in Putney and I could be in any scary city in the world.

'I said, gimme the dosh. *Now.*' Oh God, he's got my lapels. Ugly. Squinting eyes. He's virtually foaming. I'm fumbling for the money. Please don't hit me. I can't fight back. Where is it? No, they're the photos. Ah, here. Take it. Don't hit me. Anger in that face. Hatred. Good food and wine. He's looking at the wad. Aargh. Pain. Blood. The road. More pain. Thoughts random now. Can't think. Stars. Kicking. Again and again. Leg. Stomach. Warmth. Blood. Tin can. Damp. Night. Sleep.

God, I shouldn't have had that last drink. Where's the light switch? Bloody keys. Always dropping them. There's Mrs Stokes across the hall.

'Evening,' she mumbles.

Best reply, I suppose. 'Evening, Mrs Stokes.' Blimey, well slurred. Never mind. Cup of coffee for me. Damn that Stella. What a nice bird. Chatting away too. I suppose I shouldn't have belched in her face.

Where's the bloody coffee? Ah, bread. That means toast. In a bit. Kettle first. Then maybe a spot of telly before bed. Shit. Can't even hold a spoon. Turn ti tum. Music. Radio on. Michael Bolton. Radio off. Ah, kettle's finished. Must get around to painting this ceiling.

Right, living room. Bollocks. Where's the light switch? Typical. Half past two Saturday morning and the bulb goes. Pissed out of my head. Well, I'll just have to go by the light of the telly. If I can find it. Can't be arsed to find another bulb. Shit. Ah. No. Er... ah, there we are. Let's see. Hmm. ITV. Rubbish. BBC2. Subtitles. No, not now. Ow. Coffee's too hot.

What's that noise? Bit of a racket going on out there. Probably a few drunks having a row over the take-outs. Sounds like a hefty argument.

'Gimme the money.' Oooh. Could be a 'Crimewatch' job. Better have a look. Ow. Damn table. Hmm. More misty than I remember. Can't see much. Bloody hell. Look at that. Where's Mrs Stokes? Gotta get plod.

'Mrs Stokes! Mrs Stokes!' Shit, bloody table. 'Mrs Stokes!' Typical. She'll have gone to bed. Door.

'What d'you want?' Lovely dressing-gown. Glad I wasn't her husband.

'Mrs Stokes, there's some blokes having a fight in the road below. One in a raincoat beating the hell out of this scruffy git. Really serious. Ring the police.'

Looks a bit sceptical.

'Honest!'

Ah, at last. Hey, wait. She's put the latch on. Stupid cow. I can't ring in this state... they won't believe me... they won't...

I'll get that scruffy little twat if it's the last thing I do. I'll beat the living daylights out of him. What a fucking ponce. I'll beat him so he won't know his arse from his elbow. Blackmailing a member of parliament. Who the fuck does he think he is? Where the hell are we? Some fag-end of Britain, no doubt. Where no-hopers like him live. Bribe the fuck out of any police in this area. What a dick! Thinking he can arrange a meeting with me. At his time! In his place! And then he thinks he can keep the photos. Cheeky sod. Are there no people around here? I thought these squalid dives are over-run with all sorts of undesirables. Foreigners even. God, the wanker can run fast.

Ah, a park. Smaller than my front lawn probably! I'll teach him; I'll bloody teach him. Wonderful! A dead end.

'Gotchya now ya bastard.'

Look at him. Cowering, snivelling. Smelly little oik in a godforsaken alley.

'Alright you bastard... ' Oooh. Overdone the running. Bloody heart's pounding away. Ha ha, look at him! Can't even speak.

'... gimme the money.' I'll get those damned photos too. If I have to kill him for them. I might do that anyway. 'I said gimme the dosh. *Now.'* You scrawny git. I'll beat the hell out of you. I'll butt him for a start. Ah, wait. The money. All there? Hmmm. Looks like it. Right. I'll butt him anyway. And kick him a bit. Serves him right. Sack of shit. Where's the photos? All finished. Don't think I'll kill him. One more kick for good measure. There. Right. Where's a taxi? Cold night. Damp.

Ah, shit. Shit. Pain. Pain. Unbearable pain. I can't breath. I can't fucking breathe. Help.

'Help.' Too faint. 'Help.' Shit. Falling. The road. It's cold. Please God, help me. Windows. Light. Help, help. Night. Sleep.

A Twist for a Drink

by

Philip Northam

'Did you know,' asked my friend, 'that an insurance company will often pay for suicide?'

I answered that I did not, and why had he asked?

'Well, just recently, an acquaintance of mine became involved in just such a situation. Once an honest man, he had fallen on hard times. Civilised veneer shattered, he decided upon a drastic course of action to alleviate his suffering. Murder. Like all the best remedies, it kept on working.

His plan was simple. Murder someone, make it seem to be suicide, and collect the money - simple? Not really. Any insurances he had had long since vanished, cashed in his desperation for money. The only course left to him was to find an accomplice. The tricky part was finding a likely candidate with which to carry out his plan. For some time this perplexed him, though his ingenuity was fuelled by gnawing hunger. Killing a man seemed the easy part. Benefiting from his wealth was not possible... unless he could find a dissatisfied wife... '

The picture was taking shape. I leaned forward, eager for him to continue.

'Suddenly it was obvious to him what he had to do. Being a rather shy man, however, this proved to be the hardest part of his plan. You do not find a woman who wants to kill her husband on every street corner - especially when they're rich.'

My friend poured two drinks, pausing before the climax to his story. I took mine: its fire clawed in my throat.

'By complete good fortune - it seemed his first in an eon - he met a lady with a car and a coat, the former of these in need of attention. As a reward for his yeomanry, she invited him for a drink as bored housewifes are sometimes wont to do when their husbands are away. It was not hard to sense her distaste as he steered the conversation to her spouse. And a little the worse for drink, he blurted his plan out to her, preparing himself for a speedy departure. But she listened, and it was as if they shared suddenly, an amazing intensity.

And so, the plan was formed. As his part of the bargain, the husband's 'suicide' was to be effected as soon as possible. For her part, the wife would collect her substantial insurances on her husband's death. When the dust had settled, she would pay her collaborator for his services and they would go their separate ways. Free and rich. He lived for that.

Having spent some time quizzing the wife over her husband's habits, he finally decided on a course of action.

Poison.

'People have been murdered by poisoning before.' I spluttered.

'True. So a suicide note was forged - or rather, it was typed on his own office typewriter, and slipped in for him to sign with a stack of letters. He didn't notice.'

'How was he poisoned?' I asked, finishing my whisky.

'Nice drink?' He asked.

How simple he was. To fall for a trick like that. He felt smug. No one knew he had been there.

He would never forget the look on his friend's face as realisation dawned and he looked, sickened, at the moist remnants of his last drink. It was too late then - the poison had taken a grip, and his lethargic struggle proved unequal to the waves of death that pumped through his body. He departed, left him slumped in his chair, note on desk. As he closed the door behind him, the loose ends were erased.

Some months later, the grieving wife received a handsome cheque, and finally it was time for the bargain to be honoured. He waited patiently. The Police and the coroners mulled for some time before proving conclusively that suicide was indeed the sad verdict. So he asked for his money.

'Who,' asked the widow, 'would believe you? You barely know him anyway - why would you murder him. What motive would you have?'

He realised with a growing horror that having risked all, he had failed at the final hurdle. He had been crossed by this slight and scheming widow, and had no redress which would not involve his own demise. He had no standing, there was nothing he could do. Having lost all that was dear to him, he found that there was nothing to retrieve. Even his honour was now bankrupt, and he hung his head in shame.

But the shame did not last long. Soon, where it had burned, a burning brand galvanised him. All he had was his anger.

He realised there was no perfect crime. He had blood on his hands which could not be washed away. His crime of perfection had imprisoned him as surely as if he had slit his victim's throat inside a police station. There was no proof, no gain. Legally - laughed at the thought - he had no claim to the money.

As his thoughts fermented, one endured. The widow grieved with dedication, her pain seemed hard to bear. How could life continue without her husband? Thoughtfully, he poured himself a drink.

Green Twist

by

D F Lewis

Hector spent most of his waking hours doing jigsaw puzzles. It never crossed his mind that he might be wasting his life, for he found the whole activity relaxing, absorbing, generally civilised and, yes, cathartic.

He became so expert, he speedily progressed from the large chunky pieces designed for the short-witted, towards those that numbered their pieces in thousands. Then there were the ones with bits bearing malformed joints and appendages. He even had puzzles which eventually formed pictures in scales of life to life and larger...

As the carriage clock on the mantelpiece kept the silence in rigorous shape and, with the heavy-duty curtains half-pulled across the net-choked window, he propped the huge purpose-built board upon his spreading middle-aged beer-belly of a lap, emptied the contents of a wickedly difficult jigsaw into the cracked china chamber-pot beside him and proceeded to fit the whole affair together... without recourse to the picture on the box-lid and working from the middle outwards. Years of experience had made him a dab hand, as wily as a snake.

He purchased spanking new boxes from the Dickensian toy shop nearby with the big bay window. There were always stacks of them on the shelves - in fact, the place seemed to sell little else. The toothbrush-moustached shopkeeper knew Hector's little foibles very well and chose the next puzzle for him, so that Hector need not look at the box-lid. The shopkeeper was indeed one of those rare breeds who believed the customer was always right... even when he was wrong. He knew that the time was approaching when Hector would be entirely dissatisfied with straightforward jigsaws. One had to be cruel to be kind, even if it meant tempting Hector beyond the edge.

Back home, Hector excitedly stripped off the cellophane with blunt finger-nails, whilst keeping his eyes tightly averted, and poured the contents with a sensuous jiggling noise into the freshened chamber-pot.

One day, he was particularly pleased, because the shopkeeper had told him that the new puzzle had a picture that was really awe-inspiring. Something about Eve and the Tree of Knowledge. Always pleased with religious themes,

Hector was bound to be satisfied with the end result. And the box contained more pieces than any other that the shopkeeper had ever seen in his experience. No two pieces the same shape. More than life size, he wouldn't mind betting. As the innards of the clock gave out an uncharacteristic whirring, jarring noise, Hector began to pick out bits one by one from the chamber-pot. His ultimate knack was to be lucky with the first few samples. Then he built up the picture, detail by minute detail, gradually obtaining an overview of the subject-matter, colours blending, form from form, shapes born, evolving, extruding...

Today was a dark day. The sky lugubrious. The street lamps lit earlier than usual. At first, he couldn't believe the outline which was emerging upon the lap board. Snake scales. Mottled hide. Winding coils of microscopically diamond-quartered skin. Hooked teeth, whiter than he could ever credit a jigsaw reproducing. As he headed out towards the straight bits, he felt sickness constricting his throat. He couldn't account for his feelings. But, then, horror-struck, he realised there *were* no straight bits... and the chamber-pot was nearly empty.

He desperately searched for the box-lid in the gloom, finally discovering it in the coal scuttle. He barely discerned a rather picturesque view of St Paul's Cathedral, a majestic landlocked square-rigger set against the bluest sky that could only be seen in picture-books.

The contents had obviously been stashed in the wrong box.

Hector rushed over to the chamber-pot to be violently sick.

There was merely a pause for tension.

As he began to sense the pulsing spirals of slime slide up his bare leg, he remembered he had forgotten to switch on the light in his puzzle-solving haste. However, he could see that his skin was a mosaic of green scales, wet to the eye, but dry to the forked flicker of his own tongue.

He fled to the mirror... but his by now could only reflect its own darkness. He thought he must have become a monster that had only managed to escape because there were no straight bits forming the jigsaw's margins to keep it in. He spun back across the parlour on this one-leg tail and instinctively planted his fangs into his own belly, grateful that he was sufficiently double-jointed to recycle the venom.

China Girl

by

Robert Matthews

On Radio Four, 'Madam Butterfly' came through strong and clear on that cold grey December morning.

Call it fate, call it what you will, but the instant Puccini's haunting arias died away, the postman delivered a letter addressed to me from the 'People's Republic of China'.

I had fallen hopelessly in love with my 'China Girl', six months before. As things turned out, I never expected to hear from her again.

Filled with unbearable poignancy and excitement, I ripped open the envelope and withdrew Cao's letter. I thought I'd got over her, but as I began to read her painfully written words, I knew she still meant everything to me.

Cao Rong's writing was difficult to follow. In places, where her tears had fallen, the ink had run and blurred the words across the pink, feint lined flimsy sheet.

She wrote: 'Dear Mr Bob', (she'd always called me Mr Bob and I her, China Girl) 'How are you? I was hope you would send photo. The one of you and me, which Mr Ling, he took in Islamabad.

'Mr Bob, you remember your China Girl Cao? China Girl smiling? Now China Girl cry. (Here the words were barely decipherable) I am so sad today as I think of you.

'When we say goodbye that night, I ask for transfer home. Now, so sorry.

'Then, you remind me so much of boyfriend. I told you about my poet painter with long hair? You so much like him, I fall in love with you, like I tell you. Did I did not say you, he killed Tiamenen did I?

'When I meet you Mr Bob, I cannot bear. You understand? I love so much my Mr Bob. It crazy! I had to go home. Now always, please think only of your China Girl smiling. Goodbye, remember Cao your China Girl, she always love you wherever.'

That was it, one page of concentrated emotion, that left me strung out for the rest of the day, wrapped in the dreams of what might have been.

I first met Cao with her boss, Mr Ling, in a Pakistan Government travel agency in Islamabad last June. I was fixing up a trip to Pakistan's remote

166

mountainous northern areas, when Cao and Mr Ling, walked unannounced into the office.

Changez, the Manager, was helping the Chinese make a co production film for the Bureau of Tourism in Urumqui, in the Xinjian Province of China bordering on Pakistan. Ling was the head camera man and Cao his translator, who spoke some English.

Cao took little notice of the fact that Changez was on the 'phone.

'Changez!' She exclaimed petulantly, interrupting him. As she tossed her head, her black waist length hair cut a gleaming arc like a thoroughbred's, before settling back in place. 'You always on 'phone you, no time for China people.'

She stood over Changez, her endlessly long legs, encased in badly fitting cotton trousers, tapered down to small slippered feet. One of them tapped furiously, as she said, 'You bad man Changez.' Then turning in my direction, asked, 'Who this man?'

Completely captivated by her beauty, I didn't hear her at first. She was so exquisite, that I was completely thrown off balance.

She glided towards me, small pubescent breasts swinging freely beneath her sleeveless blouse. Her black almond eyes set in a flawless, pale complexioned face, instantly softened as she looked at me. For a fraction of a second, her eyes wavered with what I took to be a flicker of recognition. As quickly, it was gone, and in it's place shone an expression of delight.

'You not Pakistani?' She said, her full red lips parting in a wide smile to expose teeth like mother of pearl.

'No,' I replied, 'I'm English.'

'English! English!' She transposed her 'l's and r's' like all orientals. Only, on her the lisp sounded enchanting. 'Many English visit China, but only old men, with old wives!' Cao burst into peals of laughter and demanded, 'What you do in Islamabad?'

She listened solemnly, as I explained that I was researching a book I planned to write... Finally, she asked, 'Are you good writer?' Then flatly, 'I think you good.'

As she fixed me with her luminous eyes, I couldn't at first believe what I saw in their depths. They seemed to be filled with nothing less, than what I can only describe as love. I was smitten instantaneously, as miraculously and as inexplicably.

167

I remember babbling on like a child, talking pure gobbledeegook. She responded in Chinese, which made no sense. But in the universal language of love, sense has no place or meaning.

I can't explain how, or why it happened. I only know that Cao and I both fell in love that instant. At that moment, nothing else in the world mattered other than what we felt for each other.

We had both made a stupendous, headlong leap into the unknown, where in our magical state of enchantment Mr Ling and Changez could have been in Outer Mongolia for all we cared. It didn't even enter my reckoning that Mr Ling might have been Cao's political commissar.

I asked Cao if she'd have dinner with me that evening.

'Yes, yes, please, nine o'clock 'Flashman' Hotel.' She answered with a smile, without hesitation. I said goodbye then. As I left, I caught Mr Ling's inscrutable glance.

I was relieved to see Cao alone when I called for her. I'd half expected Mr Ling to be there. Her long cool fingers were like soft petals as she reached out to touch my face in greeting.

She was dressed in a closely fitting, shimmering green silk gown, and in her hair, she wore a pink hibiscus flower. Outside in the moonlight, she was a vision of incandescent loveliness.

We dined in a nearby Afghan restaurant. Throughout the meal we hardly spoke, and over green tea at the end of it, we held hands like children, oblivious to all around us.

When I dropped Cao outside her room, she startled me by putting her arms around my neck and kissing me gently on the lips.

'Mr Bob,' she said softly, 'I love you. Not kissy kissy love like movies. Real love, from heart.'

I hardly slept that night thinking of her. All I wanted, was to be with her always. By morning, I had convinced myself that somehow, we were going to spend our lives together, whatever our cultural differences.

At ten o'clock I asked the hotel receptionist if I could be put through to her room. He said sorry, but the Chinese crew had already left for Lahore two hundred miles away, and no, Miss Rong had not left any message. The man told me that I could find the group at Felletti's Hotel situated in the cantonment there.

It's impossible to describe my state of torment as I caught the next 'plane to Lahore. At Felletti's Hotel the receptionist told me that Miss Rong was not a guest, although the other Chinese had checked in.

Mr Ling and another, came through the lobby just as I was about to leave. Ling's companion told me that Miss Rong had flown directly home to Urumqui from Islamabad at eight that morning.

Ultimately, I gave up when I couldn't get any more information out of them, convinced that Mr Ling had been at the bottom of Cao's sudden departure. After which, heart broken, and completely decimated, I followed my original plans and spent some disconsolate weeks trekking in the Himalayas. With the certainty that I'd never hear from my 'China Girl' again, I eventually returned home to London.

Tracing my fingers over the stains left by Cao's tears, I read and re-read her letter. Finally, I knew what I had to do.

China Airlines fixed me up with a visa from their Embassy and got me a flight to Urumqui with a stopover in Beijing the following week.

I'd pulled out Cao's letter so many times to read on the twenty hour flight, that it was in tatters by the time we reached Beijing. Then on to Urumqui by another 'plane, over endless plains and snowy mountains 'till we finally arrived there five hours later.

Outside the airport, I hailed a ramshackle taxi and gave the driver Cao's Bureau of Tourism address which was written in Chinese on the back of her air letter.

The temperature was minus eighteen and it was deathly cold. The streets, piled high with snow, were flanked by post Stalinist grey apartment blocks. Nothing stirred in the grim Kafkaesque scene.

We stopped outside a garishly painted building which my driver indicated was the one I wanted.

Inside, It was unbearably hot. Peeling off my layers of clothing, I could hardly contain my excitement at the prospect of surprising my beloved Cao.

Mr Ling entered, his mouth dropping in astonishment when he saw me. He immediately retreated, to return with the English speaking Chinaman I'd met in Lahore. Mr Ling's companion put his fingers to his mouth.

'Miss Rong die ten days back,' he said, 'take pills. Now sleep with forefathers.'

Ten days back, was the date of 'China Girl's' letter.

Joy

by

David Allen

A stranger easing along that country lane nipped in between the avenue of beech trees and the broad dry stone wall twisting sluggishly over the hill, might pause to catch their breath and observe the beauty of it all. If they should stay a while they would see more flowers than they would remember, for this land was blessed. They might even see, could fate draw their stare that way, an ambling spillage of fireside smoke drift across the tree tops and blacken their leaves so that they seemed dead or dying. If you should follow the trail to its source you would find a tall chimney and a small white cottage locked within a briar embrace. A sliver of wood with knotted rope ties at either end swings above the front and only door. Printed neatly in scarlet ink, but so overcome by age it is difficult to read, is the name 'Roselea'. This is the home that George and Rosemary built.

George and Rosemary live here although many years have passed since the final stone was laid and the wooden fence pegged deep into its last resting place.

George and Rosemary are very old. George loves Rosemary.

If George was proud of anything he was proud of his love. He had sustained and nurtured it over these plentiful years. It was his love and he cherished it. 'I love you Rosemary'. He wanted to shout these words out loud until the earth shook and the trees shed their leaves. He never did. He was too cautious a man for that. He knew his place and he knew that he would never tempt fate. Fate might ruin everything and what is left after that. But George within his own parameters actively sought contentment through certain knowledge. But, knowledge or truth of themselves could never satisfy him. He wanted, in fact he craved the intimacy of touch, to spread his fingertips across the contours of those words, to caress and shelter them so that they grew and spread wild; and, every night before the mirror he watched his lips push those love words out like final farewell morsels of breath and each time the words seemed newly created, newly born. Sweet breath, he thought, as he wrote 'G loves R' in the gathered mists of condensation on the mirror before brushing them gently away.

If a stranger had spied this singular dialogue they would, or might have commented (if they didn't give George the benefit of the doubt) that he was mad. He was old enough to be mad and too old to be in love; well, George thought so anyway.

Today is a summer's day. George sits back in the chilled shadows of the apple tree. He is drinking a glass of iced lemon water. He watches courting butterflies unravel their passion through the pungent mists of pollen, clouding the early afternoon. Rosemary prefers to lie in bed. Her bed is pressed into the darkest corner furthest from the door. If you walked the stony path that wound around the cottage you might fail to see the window to Rosemary's room so high and small that it was. The absence of sunlight did not trouble her. She was attracted by the cool touch of uncertainty. There were curtains too and these were always tightly drawn. Darkness was so familiar in this room that George sometimes forgot the window and wondered how he could bring the room light.

Rosemary was so plain in rest that he sometimes wondered why he had given her a second glance. Noses were George's forte and she had a nose in youth that celebrated precision. Sadly age drew her flesh downwards into fattening wads to puff her nostrils like a cluster of bees. George did not care. He had a good memory and a kind heart. What was a nose to an old man.

Rosemary was blind. She told George that seeing did not concern her because there was nothing that she wanted to see. George wondered how she pictured him in her imagination but she wouldn't say. To Rosemary conversation was an unnecessary distraction although it was difficult to see what she was distracted from. George did not mind. He knew that they expressed themselves in different ways. He knew they understood each other well and that words were superfluous. George often thought of their conversations. He remembered them all, and liked to sift them daily to give him nourishment. Sometimes Rosemary did not say what she meant. She was more articulate than George and yet she was carefree and careless with her words. She said so few George thought it such a pity that she didn't think before she spoke. Sometimes she would tease him. George did not understand humour too well and he struggled in the search to discover what made her laugh. Sometimes she just teased him and didn't bother to laugh.

'Who are you?' She would challenge. 'What poison do you bring me?' And then there would be silence.

Poor George. Watch him staring, braced with arched back against the door. He has brought Rosemary a cup of tea and as he stirs, each slow spooned revolution spills droplet after droplet and a rich brown moat fills the saucer. Trem-

171

bling rings radiate out. He knew he would not question her, it was just not his way. He wished he knew the words to please but he had lost the confidence to talk and lost the words to say. How could he love this woman so much and yet understand her so little. Why was this woman so different from the rest. If only he understood her always there would be no sorrow. But he did not speak and his dreams tumbled from his lips and scattered like petals in a storm. Look how they fall and drift away into the dark corners of the room.

At her bedside now. He was so close he could have touched her. Rosemary turned her face to where he rested and raised her eyes to meet his. Poor Rosemary, she felt his stare as sharply as a slap and even as she averted her face a second scything blow scorched her cheeks red. Breathless, shaken, rising up and crying out. Listen to her suffering; and yet where is the blood. Did the blood come, she knew it must; and feeling rivulets of warmth steal across her cheeks she searched them out with shifting fingertips like spiders. Later she sucked them dry one by one and she knew it was not to be. There was no blood, there were no blows.

She must have control. She must have control. Rosemary closed her eyes to shut him out, to banish his shadow that dared to lay down beside her, clinging like a fever. Paralysed. Crippled. Under siege and overrun by the storm from his miserable soul. His seas rose up and swept her helplessly away to distant waters.

Now watch her slowly drown.

Her eyes are open, staring, fixed. It is almost as if she can see. Now watch her. Watch her drown. Flooding lungs. Flailing arms, stretching, pleading up to God, gagging on salt and seaweed, and sand, and spit. She is drowning. Watch her try to say goodbye. She is dead.

'Fuck you, George,' she whispered and brushed the fire from her lips. She turned to confront and contemplate this man, this face, the eyes, the mouth, the nose and then she spat at his weakness and drew in huge whale gulps of his life and pulled it tight into her mouth and pressed the sweetness into her flesh, counting back his years of suffering. She pictured a barren field and threw him in it, alone, isolated, helpless. And then, for every day of their shared misery (and she laughed at that) she gave him a stone and with these stones she built a wall. A wall so tall she lost sight of it in the clouds and with this wall she divorced herself from George. She could not see him now but that was not enough, and so she blew the wall down so that she would never see him again.

Rosemary could not repress her smile.

George loved Rosemary.

172

The Reunion

by

Rosalee Green

I had not seen her for, well, it must be thirty years or more. She had moved away after we left school, and although we had been good friends, the friendship had not extended to corresponding with each other, but I had thought about her often. She was still fair, pretty, thinner than I. In fact she looked quite skinny; taut, it seemed. Perhaps it was aerobics, the cult now with housewives. I was too idle to participate in anything so strenuous - golf was my game. So there we were, trolleys interlocked and profusely apologising - until,

'Deidre', I gasped, 'It can't be!'

'It is', she replied, 'How marvellous to see you, Angela, after all these years. I recognised you instantly; you've hardly changed at all.'

We disengaged our heaped trolleys.

'Let's get out of here and have some coffee,' I said.

We waited in the queue impatiently, both eager to question the other.

'How long has it been?' I asked.

'At least thirty years,' we agreed simultaneously.

I eyed her trolley surreptitiously. Coffee, milk, cheese, pizzas, some TV meals and oven chips. Perhaps her family was still at home. I had a couple of chickens and some barbecue steaks for the weekend if the weather held, and fruit and party bits and pieces.

'How is it we haven't met sooner?' Asked Deidre. 'Do you live nearby?'

'Just around the corner, actually, *on* the corner.'

'What, that lovely big house with the beautiful garden and the frilly drapes!' She almost shrieked.

Well, I suppose it is rather attractive - I've always been told I have good taste, and especially since we changed the front door to oak and fixed two very smart coach lamps. John has a good executive post and he likes everything - traditional.

I asked Deidre where she lived.

'The other end of this road, in Davenport Street,' she replied.

I knew it, rather poky little houses, but quite neat with small front gardens.

'Bob has a new job now, but his boss is very autocratic so he is under a great deal of stress; the salary isn't worth the worry, but at least Bob's working. I'm glad the children are off hand, married and living away.'

She had two children, as I had, but mine are still at university. John always believed in a sound education. We came out and I loaded my car which had a capacious boot, and waited for Deidre. We were going for coffee in a nearby lounge and her Mini followed my Golf GTI.

'I can't stay long,' said Deidre. 'Bob comes home for lunch and he barely has an hour. His boss usually has an extended lunch hour, but he seems to know who is back late. I expect his secretary tells him. I've said, if he wants to leave, we'll manage for a bit. Bob's not used to feeling persecuted, he calls it.'

She became pensive for a moment, then sighed and said, 'We must be thankful though, but I do feel Bob's worth and his true potential are not fully recognised.'

I felt sorry for them. We paused our chatting while we drank our coffee and I was glad I'd ordered tea-cakes. John in his position has to keep a very firm hand on the staff. He often tells me the new men don't have the experience nor the enthusiasm to learn and that's why he's an executive and they are still on the bottom rung. I mused on this and felt sympathy for Deidre and her Bob.

'Of course we've only been here for a few months,' she said, 'which is probably why we haven't bumped into each other - literally - before; we don't get out much.'

'You must come over for dinner one evening,' I said. 'John gets home from Lelands about seven. We can have a nice chat about old times and... '

'Lelands!' Cried Deidre, a look of horror on her face. 'That's my Bob's firm, your husband must be John Brownlow!'

She was very red and I felt hot and bothered.

'Please, please don't repeat what I said - I had no idea and Bob does try so hard.'

'I never interfere in John's business affairs,' I assured her.

Her pretty face looked near to tears. She really hadn't changed much, just that she looked rather defeated, I suppose. I knew we wouldn't come together again, there would be a natural resentment and I couldn't handle it. We both stood up and she rummaged in her handbag for her keys.

'I must get home for Bob's lunch - it was nice seeing you again, Angela.'

'Yes, rather, you too. We must visit soon.'

But we both knew it wouldn't happen.

Last Love

by

Daniel Coxon

Alex took the stub from the man at the door and walked in, thrusting it carelessly into one of his inside pockets. A fine tobacco mist had settled over the hall, drifting on a plane a few feet above the obscured seated forms, merging them into a collage of colours on the floor. Occasionally a clustered group of standing figures broke through the smoke clouds, hands clutching desperately at half-empty plastic glasses as they tried to talk above the music crashing from the speakers, lip-reading becoming a necessary skill.

Picking his way carefully through the maze, occasionally having to retrace his steps or force a path between embracing couples, he made his way towards the front. There was a strong smell of beer, sweat and tobacco here, the aftermath of the support act; he'd been working too late to be able to catch them, but the row he'd heard from outside as they'd wound up hadn't shown much promise. It was Three Day Growth he'd really come to see, anyhow; this was the second time he'd been to one of their concerts, the first had been at Glastonbury, and if that was anything to go by tonight was going to be divine.

The lights were beginning to dim as he checked his shoelaces and readied himself for the surge, the seated groups standing up and pushing forwards as they realised the show was about to start. Packed in from all sides, Alex began to feel a little claustrophobic, the thick air stifling in his lungs and threatening to open his stomach. As sweat broke on his forehead he tried desperately to keep it down, already faint with the effort: someone had thrown up on him once at Reading, and it wasn't a nice experience. Trapped in by the darkness as much as the blackly solid forms about him, he suddenly became aware of the fact that there was no way out anymore, the crowd packing the hall from wall to wall; but then the stage lit up, throwing its pale, unearthly glow over the seething sea of people, and with a drum roll that heralded their presence the music began.

As the initial wave of guitar noise erupted from the speakers the crowd about him began to bob up and down, his feet automatically matching their rhythm, only slightly out of time with the bass drum on the stage. The couple in front of him began to sway from side to side, allowing him lightning glimpses of the bright flashes up front, but he was too engrossed in the tender rhythms of the music to notice.

At the time it seemed only minutes into the concert that he noticed her, but looking back it must have been almost an hour. It was in between songs, amidst squeals and wolf-whistles from the crowd, that he turned his head and his eyes fixed upon her face. Her eyelids were open but the pupils dilated, matted strands of sweat-darkened hair clinging like seaweed to her forehead. Her body was pressed close against his by the force of the crowd, her flesh warm through his shirt; yet, despite their nearness, he was afraid to touch her, to do anything but smile and turn back to the stage, cursing inwardly at his cowardice.

Then another pounding bass riff announced the start of the next song, and his feet once more left the ground as the crowd began to dance, but by now that slim, pale face was imprinted on his mind, and he thought only of keeping as close as possible to the warmth of her flesh. In the next interval he turned to introduce himself, but his words were lost amongst the shouts from the crowd: she was probably too stoned to hear anyway. Instead he just let his eyes rest upon her features once more, this time allowing every little detail to seep in and lodge in his mind. Under the pure, fluorescent light from the stage her face was unblemished, the earthly embodiment of marble-carved Aphrodite. Her dilated pupils and far-away look only added to the effect; aloof and serene she became a goddess in her own right.

As he stood watching her a faceless black form pushed past, sending her body reeling into the person in front, Alex's arm catching her just in time to stop her from crumpling to the floor. Her back was wet-probably spilt beer or sweat, the alternative didn't bear thinking about - but even as the music started up again, the band playing one of his favourites as a first encore, his arm stayed where it was, supporting her limp body. This was the reason he could never bring himself to smoke that stuff; his mind was what guaranteed his future, and even temporary loss of control brought up an infinity of horrors. He liked to think that he had a pretty free attitude towards drugs, but they weren't for him.

Eventually the song came to a close, and he turned to look at her face again. It was perfectly still, the few beads of sweat on her forehead glistening like pearls. He'd be the first to admit that he hadn't had much success with women - after all, he'd only properly dated twice in his entire life - but he'd always held out that it was only because he hadn't met the ideal women: now he held her in his arms he knew that he'd been right. As soon as she came out of her drugged stupor she'd fall instantly in love with him, he could picture it even now.

The concert had finished and people were beginning to move off, but he remained where he was, arm tightly clutching tonight's prize, his lifetime partner. Leaning over he whispered an almost inaudible 'I love you' as he planted a tender kiss on her pale cheek, his contented smile turning into a grimace of horror and disgust as the house lights came on and he drew away his red-stained hand, watching wide-eyed as her corpse thudded to the floor to lie in a pool of spilt beer and spent fag-ends.

And when he screamed he almost woke the dead.

Alex got off the train at a quarter to midnight and walked clumsily down the steps to the street below. A businessman and an old lady got off at the same time, but he ignored them and they were soon lost to the night as he started up the hill towards his flat.

The Police doctor - what did you call them, pathologists? - had said she'd been dead for almost an hour, probably not long after the concert started: one knife wound to the back, penetrating something vital on the way in. Her body had been kept upright by the force of the crowd: and his arm, of course. They'd cleaned the blood from his shirt as soon as possible, but the dampness still served as a reminder as he trudged wearily home. It was unlikely they'd find her killer.

Why? of all people, why her? He'd never known her, in life that is, but she'd seemed so kind, so beautiful... He felt like crying, but generations of male inbreeding held the tears back.

Now the only sounds were the dull thuds as his feet struck tarmac, matching the unnatural rhythm of his heart: even the bats were asleep. He began to draw his hand across his lips, then stopped himself with an unspoken reprimand. He hadn't known she was dead, it wasn't his fault; her body was still clean anyway, fresh, there was nothing to be ashamed of. Yet, as he walked on, her face stared serenely at him from out of the shadows, and for once his feet felt the bodies through the tarmac and earth.

His finals began in two days, but revision could wait. Tonight he intended to get very drunk.

The Lodger

by

Jim Purdy

'You could make me a cup of tea before you go out, Susan.'

Susan snapped her handbag shut in annoyance. 'Mother, wheelchair or not, you're perfectly capable of making a pot of tea yourself, so let's not start that nonsense. Since the lodger moved in upstairs you haven't given me a minute's peace, and don't forget, having a lodger was your idea in the first place. And another thing, Mother, the forty pounds a week is more than welcome. The bills are not getting any smaller, and this year we have the added horror of Poll Tax, remember?'

'Huh! Look at you now, Susan. Dressed like a duchess. If you ask me the lodger's rent is going on new clothes. That's another new costume you're wearing isn't it?'

'Mother I got this suit for half-price in the January sales, plus a few other things which I badly needed. Why don't you mention the years I've denied myself? The years spent waiting on you hand and foot. Yes, since Dad died twenty years ago. And now when I've a chance to go out for an evening, to enjoy myself, you spoil it by complaining.'

'Huh! You're going out three nights a week. I hardly ever see you now.'

'Mother, say what you like, I don't care. If I feel like it, I'll go out every night. So there!'

'Huh! I wonder what the neighbours think.'

'You can 'Huh' all you like, Mother. And the neighbours can 'Huh' too. It's my life and I'm going to enjoy what few years I've got left.'

'I'm ashamed Susan. I really am.'

'Well, I'm not, Mother, so shut up.'

'I think I'll sell the house and go into an Old People's Home.'

'Why don't you, Mother? I'll not stand in your way. My conscience is clear.'

'I'll sell the house and take the money with me. You'll not get a penny, Susan.'

'If that's your way of saying 'Thanks', Mother, after my years of nursing you, then so be it. Mr Crawford, the manager at the Department Store, is more than

178

eager for me to work full-time. He has always fancied me, Mother. Haven't I told you that more than once?'

'If you were going out with Mr Crawford I wouldn't mind, but you're not, are you Susan? You're co-habiting with that thing upstairs.'

'Oh yes, Mother, it would be okay in your eyes to have an affair with Mr Crawford, wouldn't it? And him with a wife and three children at home. Well, Mr Crawford and family aren't my idea of happiness, so there.'

'Huh! Go to hell, Susan. You always were an odd bitch.'

'Point taken Mother,' Susan called back before slamming the door on her way out.

It was two minutes to eleven when Susan arrived for work. The Department Store was busy as she made her way to the staff changing room.

'Good morning Susan.'

Susan knew the voice before she looked around to greet Mr Crawford. He had a name in the store for being a womaniser. His slim, six-foot frame and easy out-going manner always put the staff at their ease; and he was liked throughout the store by all who served under his seemingly unflappable nature.

'Good morning Mr Crawford,' Susan replied, smiling.

'Mr Crawford! Mr Crawford!' he mimicked. 'Susan, how many times have I told you? Liam is my name. Mister makes me feel ancient. You know perfectly well I've only just left school.'

Susan smiled. 'Yes Mr Crawford. We all know when you left school. With Tom Brown wasn't it?'

Mr Crawford pretended to look hurt before laughing. 'Susan,' he said seriously. 'Lately I've noticed a change in your personality. You seem to be glowing; you're radiant. You exude happiness. Your bearing, your whole manner and appearance gives off this wonderful feeling of being alive. What's the secret? Please tell me. And while you're at it, tell me when you're going to say yes to our first date. The wife knows I always work late Thursdays,' he enthused with a smile.

'Mr Crawford, there are days when it's a pleasure to come in to work - this is one of them. There's no big secret; mind you, I have met someone who has changed my life. Does that answer your question?'

'No Susan, no. It can't be true,' Mr Crawford said, pretending to cry into his handkerchief. 'Does that mean I'm getting the big E?'

'Yes Mr Crawford. It's the big E for thee,' Susan said laughingly.

'Who's the lucky devil?' Mr Crawford asked, adding 'I'm insanely jealous Susan. I mean it too,' he said deadpan.

'So is Mother,' Susan answered with a frown.

'Yes of course, your mother. How is she, Susan?'

'Like I said, jealous, very jealous.'

'I can imagine,' Mr Crawford said thoughtfully, fingering his tie. 'Oh well,' he said with resignation, 'now that I know I'm not in the running for your affections, the store seems a distinctly dismal place to be. You've positively spoiled my day.'

'Look on the bright side, Mr Crawford, I could be asking you for full-time employment shortly, couldn't I?'

'I am all ears Susan,' he said,

'Mother's threatening to sell the house and disinherit me.'

'Is she? The ungrateful old bat. Forgive me Susan, I shouldn't have said that. It's none of my business.'

'No worries, Mr Crawford. You're right, of course. Mother is ungrateful.'

'Still, Susan, your mother's loss will be our gain. Just imagine having you here all day. It's the next best thing to having you home all night.'

'Now Mr Crawford!'

'I know Susan. You'd better get changed or you'll be late at the counter, Susan.'

'And who will be to blame, Mr Crawford?'

'I'll catch you later Susan.' Mr Crawford waved his hand merrily in the air as he moved off.

'Here, there's your dinner Mother. Now shut up. You're going on and on and on and on. You're just out to spoil my evening again, aren't you? You're making my life a misery. I'm losing every vestige of respect that I ever had for you, and I mean that. Do you hear?'

'Huh! Respect. That goes for you too Susan. The difference is, I'm not losing it, I've already lost it.'

'You're a cantankerous old woman. You wouldn't recognise happiness if it came up and kicked your backside.'

'Huh! Happiness: that's a new name for it. Your lodger will be pleased to hear you say that.'

'Correction Mother, our lodger; and damn lucky to have one, considering we live out in The Bush.'

'Huh! Your lodger has a car; or should I say your lover has a car? That makes life easier for you both, doesn't it?'

'Yes Mother, I was wondering when you'd get round to the word Lover. The car is a Godsend and so is my Lover. At forty six years of age it's time I shed my inhibitions. I'm grabbing life with both hands, and I'm going to hold it firmly, until eternity. Now, have you got that?'

'Huh! Well eternity can't come quick enough for me.'

'Don't show your sympathy ticket to me Mother. We've been through all this before. You know where your tablets are; take the whole bloody lot. You're getting to be impossible lately.'

'Huh! You'd like that Susan. That would simplify things, wouldn't it? You make me sick.'

'No Mother, I don't. You make yourself sick. You're green with envy. You've never cared for anyone but yourself.'

Susan applied her make-up in the mirror, and rolled her lips together to distribute the purple lipstick. Her eyes were angry. She could see her mother eating her dinner through the mirror reflection. She picked up her coat and brushed it down with her hand before putting it on. Footsteps could be heard coming down the stairs. There was a gentle knock on the door.

'Huh! Your lover awaits you Susan.'

'Come in,' Susan called eagerly.

The door opened, Cynthia stood poised in the doorway. She looked very attractive in her pleated black skirt and white blouse.

'Are you ready, Susan?' she asked, with a loving smile.